Firestorm Rising

by

John Clewarth

To Tamika,

Would love you
to write a review for
me, when you've
read my spooky book.
An best wishes,

John Clewarth
x

Written in English (UK)
ISBN: 978 – 1 – 4710 – 3681 - 1
Published by Mauve Square Publishing.

John dedicates this book to Ann, Ben and Sam.

With love and thanks.

More praise for Firestorm Rising!

"A game of hide 'n' seek in a moonlit graveyard turns into a nightmare for Tom and his friends, Jazz and Doc, after a freak fire-storm unleashes an evil from long-dead, ancient, alien bones ... bones of a creature who bends Jazz to her will with a strange pendant that the girl finds in the graveyard. Atmospheric from the start, Firestorm Rising will captivate young readers, and chill their imaginations, in an awesome tale of three children's struggle against an unearthly force. And just when you think it's all over and the darkness destroyed ... well, there just has to be a sequel somewhere out there!"

Oliver Eade, author of *Moon Rabbit*, a winner of the WAAYB 2007 New Novel Competition.

"A hair-raising story with a blend of aliens, monsters and kids that will keep you hooked until the very last page!"

Marie Godley, author of *Guardian of the Globe, Time Slide,* and the forthcoming teen novel, *Janalya.*

Firestorm Rising

by

John Clewarth

Prologue

The meteor sizzles through the vastness of space like a giant, blazing phoenix.

Flames trail behind it, ribbons of terrible heat, as it hurtles into Earth's atmosphere. The sky splits open with the thundery noise – sonic boom, gone mad.

And the sun hides behind a cloud.

* * *

The Caveman runs through the thick roots and leaves of the steaming, prehistoric jungle. His knuckles are white, clutching his long, flint-tipped spear.

Sweating.

Panting.

He has been fishing. He fishes every day. Expert at spiking the big fishes with his deadly weapon. Now, he is the hunted. He had heard the Stegosaurus before he had seen it. Heard the pounding footsteps. Felt the ground shake. Watched the fish dart away as the water broke into huge ripples.

Then it had crashed through the trees.

Now it pursues him, demolishing branches and vegetation. The Caveman dodges, twists and jumps. His heart pounds like a hammer in his chest. The Steg's thick, stumpy legs move remarkably quickly – and it is closing the distance on its prey. The Caveman stumbles on, entering a clearing now, not daring to look back. If he can make it to his cave, he knows he will be safe. He can't see the cave, but he knows it is behind the trees at the far edge of this clearing. He *must* reach it.

The Stegosaurus roars. The Caveman can smell its stinking breath; it is so close behind him. He is only a few strides from safety, when the trees are torn and splintered like matchsticks. His eyes widen, bulging with fear, as he sees the cause of this. The massive Tyrannosaurus Rex tramples over the fallen trunks as if they are grass stalks.

And it sees him.

For an instant, all three stop: Caveman, Steg, T. Rex. Then the two dinosaurs charge - straight at each other. The Caveman is stuck in the middle. He closes his eyes and waits for death. Predatory feet pound. Huge bellows signal even bigger trouble. Terrible gnashing fangs clatter and clack.

Then – nothing.

The Caveman wonders if he is dead. There is no pain at all. He opens his eyes. And he is puzzled. The giant reptiles have stopped. Both dinosaurs are close enough to reach out their slavering jaws and devour him - but they are still and silent, looking up at the sky, dagger teeth dripping. Their heads are cocked on one side.

The sky cracks, like a pterodactyl shell. The heavens growl.

The end comes fast, as the great burning rock shoots to Earth, swifter than the hunter's spear ever travelled. With a colossal thud, the

Caveman and his pursuers are obliterated, as the rock-from-the-sky pummels into the ground. The air is filled with the screeching of thousands of smaller creatures - the lucky ones – as they scatter and flee; some running, some flying, some slithering. If they turn back, they will see the deep, flaming hole in the ground.

They don't. They're too afraid.

The meteor still burns and crackles in the prehistoric soil, spitting and roaring, as if angry at being there. And smoke billows out in a towering column, like a pointing finger that threatens revenge.

Chapter 1

"… 48, 49, 50! Coming, ready or not!"

Tom Allerton uncovered his eyes and peered around him in the gloom. He loved this place, with its crumbling old tombstones, its overgrown, twisting gravel pathways and its knotty, tangled trees. Everything about Raingate Cemetery was *ancient*.

There was a large slice of moon on that late October night but the wind was up; dark clouds scuttled across the sky and sprawling oaks waved their branches like ghostly arms. Tom savoured the delicious spooky feeling in his stomach as he crept along, ankle-deep in grass, avoiding the tell-tale crunchiness of the gravel paths.

The big stone wall surrounding the graveyard cast huge shadows that mingled with the weird shapes of broken plaster angels, mouldy marble crosses and tombs the size of buses.

Tom leaned against the rugged trunk of a tree, whose branches clashed and thrashed like battling ghouls. The light quality was dim and murky tonight and, try as he might, he couldn't see anything clearly. In the distance, the ruins of Sandal Castle, though barely visible, resembled a huge, dark, burial mound. Everything was blackly-blurred round the edges; even the old house at the far end, just beyond the wall. Jazz's house. Tonight it looked like a gigantic vampire, poised and ready to spring over the cemetery wall.

"Excellent!" he whispered to himself, as the thrill-feeling fluttered through him again. This was the perfect place for hide 'n' seek with Jazz and Doc. Jazz was lucky; she was allowed to use the spare room at the very top of the house – the attic – as her den. Two things made this room good: it was huge *and* it overlooked the entire graveyard. They wouldn't have been allowed to play in here otherwise – so he guessed they were all pretty lucky.

Tom tiptoed away from the tree – and almost yelled out loud as an owl screeched nearby. Taking a deep breath and gathering his wits again, he flitted across the ground, dodging past uneven graves, peeping behind each one as he passed, hoping to see his friends crouching there in defeat.

A sound. Off to his right, between the flaking stone cuboids of two long-forgotten tombs. There, the grass was longer - waist high. It was tangled too, with nettles and all manner of other strange weeds, which nodded and squirmed in the dim light. It wasn't the whispering of the weeds that he heard though. It was a scraping sound. A scratching sound.

And was that a grunt? Surely Doc – even Jazz -wouldn't be wacky enough to hide out in a nest of stinging nettles?

He darted forward and squatted behind an arch-shaped gravestone, big enough to give him complete cover.

He hid. And he listened.

From here, he could clearly see Jazz's house - bulbous and ghoulish – lurking in the gloom. As the wind whipped up anew, he imagined the house was hissing evilly at him. He sometimes wished his imagination would not be so creative!

The clouds overhead parted in the dusk, revealing the faded lettering of the gravestone behind which he hid, in a glimmer of moonlight: Harriet Benson, aged 79. Her light now shines in Heaven.

Then the clouds ganged together again, to shut the moonlight down – and another light appeared, high up and ahead of Tom. An unsettling thought swooped into his brain. *The light. Could it be Harriet Benson? Coming to haunt him... With "her light now shining"...*

A scrabbling sound invaded his thoughts. It was coming from the nettle-infested gap between the tombs. He felt suddenly very scared. His heart started thumping harder. He wanted to finish the game right now.

"Hey, you two!" he half-shouted, half-whispered, staying crouched behind Harriet's stone. "Hey! Come out – I give up, okay?" He sat dead still and strained to hear some sign of them.

There was that grunting sound again. He wanted to say: *Pack it in, you pair of idiots!* But he couldn't make his voice work. The light up ahead caught his attention again. It seemed to be flickering.

Oh God – what's going on..?

Then he realised, with a great gasping sigh of relief, what it was. As he focused on the light, he saw that it wasn't in the sky. But it *was* high up! It was the attic room light of Jazz's house! And waving from the window, with big silly smiles on their faces, were Jazz and Doc! The pratty pair had sneaked straight out of the graveyard while he'd been counting to fifty!

He should've been mad, but he couldn't help laughing, as they jumped up and down, grinning at their own practical joke. Anyway, he knew he'd think of something to get them back. As he smiled and waved up at them, he called out, "Okay! It's a fair cop!" Though there was no chance they could have heard him.

But… *something heard him…*

A sudden flurry in the nettles; like something had scrabbled to its feet, and was now standing stock-still in the darkness. In his mind's-eye, he pictured some shapeless, hideous beast, with razor-sharp fangs, drooling hungrily. Silently watching him. Ready to pounce.

Sweat trickled down his back, even though the night was chilly. His throat was dry. He couldn't swallow. He knew he must escape. But that would mean leaving the safety of Harriet's tombstone…

He slowly, shakily, got to his feet. Silence. Except for the now howling wind that rattled the trees and whined through the cracks in the tombs. He kept his eyes on the swishing nettles between the two big tombs where the scrabbling had come from. He backed quietly away to where he knew the exit must be. About twenty metres away. Each backward step to freedom seemed to take a lifetime. He glanced up again at the attic room window and saw that Jazz and Doc were now standing still.

Did they, too, sense that something was wrong?

Tom took another step back. The damp, twitching grass seemed to be grasping at his ankles. He looked once more at the wildly weaving weeds that hid the *thing* from his view. No sound came from there.

Then –

On his next step back, his trainer-heel hit the gravel path. To Tom, the resulting noise sounded like an earthquake.

He froze.

He held his breath.

And the creature shot out of the nettles like a bat out of Hell.

Chapter 2

Kerra – i – ngg!

The room almost shook with the screaming of Doc's electric guitar. He stood with one foot propped on a low stool, twanging away at the metal strings, with a look on his face like he was sucking a sour lemon. This was his "heavy metal rock star" face.

Doc had always wanted to grow his hair long, so he could look like Marilyn Manson (he said). But every time he tried, it just sort of frizzed out like a dandelion clock. His mum told him it was just his hair-type. So now he kept it short – and it really suited him. Doc's parents had emigrated from Jamaica ten years ago, when he was born, because his dad got an important job at Leeds University.

He was nicknamed "Doc" partly because of that, and partly because of the fact that he was mad-crazy on Dr Who!

Thud – a – thud – a – thud – a! Jazz walloped the drum kit like there was no tomorrow. Her multi-coloured hair stood out at spiked angles and her eyes were closed as she whacked and bashed the skins and cymbals.

Tom tapped his foot and gripped the mike, as he peered out the attic window at the graveyard down below. He grinned as he remembered how the last game of hide 'n' seek had ended. The fox had bolted out from the nettles and away into the night, clearly more scared of Tom than he was of it. At the time, he hadn't known whether to laugh or cry, but he sure did run! He had run out of the cemetery gate and away up the road and he hadn't stopped until he'd arrived, panting and sweating at Jazz's front door. He'd got them back for their little hide 'n' seek prank by, a) nicking the strings off Doc's guitar and b) putting a white sheet over his head and sneaking up behind Jazz before rehearsal one night. She'd said she wasn't scared – but Tom didn't believe her; he'd seen her eyes popping out of her head.

He belted out the lyrics of their song:

Creeping out of an icy tomb,

The zombie's dressed to kill.

I sit and hide, in my bedroom.

Find me there – I know he will!

He was lead singer for the band and he'd written this one himself – *Zombie Rampage*. His dad said he reckoned it might never make number one, but he said he liked it anyway. And that was good enough for Tom.

As he sang, he continued to gaze out of the window at the enormous cemetery. He loved this place; and he loved this band, with his two best friends in it.

Later, when they'd finished, they crashed down on the beanbags, feeling tired but good, as they swigged Coke together.

"Ready for the big night, tomorrow?" Tom asked, his blond hair flopping over one eye.

Jazz smiled, "Yeah. What you guys coming as?"

"Guess!" Tom raised his eyebrows, eyes twinkling.

"Zombie…" Doc drawled, pretending to yawn.

"Yay, you! You're right!" Tom laughed.

Jazz chuckled and queried, "How about you, Doc?"

He put a finger to his chin, in a mock-think. "We-ell. Let's put it this way; it involves loads and loads of bandages." Doc stuck his arms out stiffly in front of him and moaned spookily.

"Mummy!" Jazz and Tom yelled at the same time.

"Jinx!" Jazz hissed, and pointed at Tom, giggling.

"So, how about you?" Doc said to Jazz, who was busy looking smug, while Tom made faces at her.

She grinned, throwing her arms out dramatically: "Ban-shee, bay-bee!!"

The room darkened a little as she spoke these words; like the energy had been drained from the lights. Then everything brightened again. "See – the darkness beckons!" Jazz declared theatrically.

With that, they all raised their cans, as Tom announced: "To Halloween!"

"To Halloween!" the others echoed.

And the trees waved madly in the graveyard, beyond the window, as if in urgent, frantic warning.

Chapter 3

Halloween had dawned dark, damp and blustery. It had stayed dark all day, but the rain had subsided and the wind had eased to nothing more than an icy breeze. When the youngsters had met in the graveyard after their 'Trick-or-Treating', complete with pumpkin lanterns, the first thing they did was compare the sweet treats they had gathered on their travels. There were eight of them altogether; three groups, all from Class 6 at Raingate Primary. Tom and Doc had formed their own little group. Most of the kids didn't think that anything was suspicious by the fact that Jazz was missing. She'd been complaining of a dodgy tummy all day at school, so she was unable to make her favourite night of the year; and it was a Friday too! Tom and Doc, however, shared the occasional secretive smile.

They looked a strange sight – vampires, ghouls, ghosts and all manner of beasties – as they sat in the middle of the cemetery, scoffing chocolate and candy. It was just as well that old Harriet Benson was tucked up mouldily in her cold stone tomb. What ever would she have made of this..?

They guffawed as they swapped silly jokes and told corny ghost stories; nobody daring to admit that they felt just a tiny bit scared - a tiny bit worried that *something* might be lurking in the thick branches of the skeletal trees, or lying in wait behind the ancient gravestones.

With fingers sticky and indigestion threatening, the eight friends sat down on the cold grass in a circle, for what was to be the high spot of the night. Lying flat on the ground, at the centre of the group, was a weathered gravestone, so old that the lettering was unreadable. In the middle of this aged stone was placed a carved pumpkin head, whose candle sent flickering shadows dancing spookily around the group, like the ghosts of the dead…

"If anyone wants to leave – if anyone hasn't the courage to see this through – then now is the time to go," Tom eerily whispered, resisting the urge to burst out laughing at what he knew was coming. Jazz had dreamed up the best practical joke ever! They were to hold a 'séance' - a calling up of the spirits from their misty world, to come and communicate with the living. And at the right time, Jazz would leap out from behind the massive tomb that was just a few metres to the left!

Tom put on his best 'horror film voice' and said, "Very well. Then let us join hands and summon the dead!" The schoolfriends reached out and held hands, hearts beating a bit quicker than normal. As if on cue, a chill wind started disturbing the branches of the old oak overhead, and clouds smothered the moon's light. The friends grasped hands more tightly. A roll of thunder grumbled faintly in the distance.

'This is great!' thought Tom, and Doc's sparkling eyes reflected the thought. *'We couldn't have hoped for anything better than this!'*

As planned, Tom uttered the predictable, but unavoidable words: "Is there anybody there?"

Silence. Followed by a flash of lightning, that seemed to be right

13

over their heads, bathing the scene in a pool of icy light. The looks on the faces of those not in on the joke were really funny; their eyes were shining with terror! Even Tom himself felt a bit apprehensive, as Doc started to moan and roll his eyes up in their sockets as they had plotted, and the thunder – louder this time – complained, uncomfortably nearby.

Doc's body shuddered, and he squeezed harder on the hands of the kids on either side, just for effect. "OOOHH!!" he groaned, to the accompaniment of gasps from the rest of the group.

"What's wrong with him?" squeaked Jenny Naylor, as the pumpkin candle flame twisted wildly in the breeze.

"I am the spirit of Martha Mallory…" Doc intoned in delicious gothic voice. "And I shall drag myself from the grave this night, and walk among you. YOU, who have called me forth!"

This was Jazz's cue to come stumbling out from the gravestones and tombs, screaming the banshee scream, to go with her wicked costume. But what happened next shocked everyone – including the tricksters, Tom and Doc.

And Jazz.

A jagged streak of lightning snaked down from the troubled sky and struck the graveyard about thirty metres from where the group sat. A deafening crack, followed by clouds of dust and showers of falling stone, as if it was raining gravel. Then the thunder came again, like an angry ogre, and the children leapt to their feet and ran – totally forgetting the pumpkin as they belted for the exit gate. They yelped and howled their fear as they stampeded out of the cemetery.

All except one. And even Tom and Doc were unaware that Jazz was nowhere to be seen.

Chapter 4

Jazz had been waiting excitedly behind a rectangular wreck of a tombstone, just a few metres away from the gathering when the lightning had struck. Upon hearing the rip-roaring impact, she had no thoughts of running away. On the contrary, her feelings of excitement escalated to pure thrill – and she sprang unseen into a sprint, straight for the location of the smoking strike.

Great plumes of foggy powder swirled about in the weird half-light around the smashed-up sepulchre that had taken the hit. Jazz skidded to a halt, so hard her trainers nearly caught fire. What had, a few seconds earlier, been a massive sarcophagus, had now become a demolition job. She peered hard, trying to focus her eyes on detail. Something deep inside her found the sight utterly fascinating. The lichen-covered, pock-marked old stone lay heaped up in jagged jigsaw chunks, all randomly stacked and seemingly ready to topple at any moment. But what Jazz *really* wanted to see – what she *really* wanted to catch a glimpse of – was what had been sealed up in there all those years ago.

She wanted to see the body. Or at least a bit of it. But strain her eyes as she might, she could see nothing, other than rubble, dust and old leaves.

And darkness.

She dropped to her knees to see more closely. And it was then that she saw – or *thought* that she saw – an eerie, inexplicable light; very faint, and of a pale luminescent purple colour. It was lurking right in the dark heart of the ruined tomb.

Jazz felt strange. Kind of dizzy. She had the oddest feeling of being *sucked in* by this unearthly light. Part of her mind screamed 'run away!' but the more insistent part of her mind urged her to stay; to find out what this thing was. She had the outlandish impression of staring into another world, another *universe*, as the lilac light shimmered. She felt small - whilst the light seemed huge. Cosmic.

Something beyond her control caused her to reach out her right hand. She leaned forward, extending her fingers towards the glow. At that precise moment, she would have happily fallen headlong into that vast, unknown cosmos. She was mesmerized.

Then her hand met with something hard and cold; part bone, part metal…

Almost with a life of their own, her fingers closed around the mysterious object. It was as if the spell had been broken. She blinked. Shook her head. And she withdrew her hand, to examine what she had grasped. As she opened her hand, palm upwards, the clouds parted in the sky - as if by magic - to expose her curiosity-piece to the moon and all the stars in the sky. In that split-second, she saw that she held what looked like a chunk of bone – *small, skull-shaped!* - attached to a gold-coloured chain that was remarkably shiny to say that it had been buried for so many years. The chain glistened like golden fire and the weird bony lump felt like a chunk of ice in her hand. She shivered, and stuffed the object into the pocket of her black jeans.

Suddenly, she wanted to find her friends again. Wanted to be out of this place. She turned and began walking quickly away. She felt disorientated and had the most awful feeling that she was being *watched.*

She broke into a steady run. The wind had whipped itself into panic and the naked trees stretched their spindly fingers in an effort to grab her. The whole *graveyard* seemed to be spinning around her, like a Victorian zoetrope, conjuring twisted, ghastly images.

Then she became aware of the smell. Yet it was more than a smell: it was a *stench* like nothing she'd ever encountered before. She wanted to be sick. She stopped and doubled over, hands on her knees, gasping. Her mind rattled like an overloaded computer, as her brain tried to figure what the smell could be. *It was like a mixture of...*

The thought withered and died in her head as the black night was shattered into a thousand fragments by the ear-splitting sound that came from the sky itself; an awesome, deafening *screech* that rode on the back of the screaming wind and got inside her head, burning like acid.

Heart hammering, she straightened and clapped her hands over her ears. The noise acted like a trigger and she ran, hell-for-leather.

When she reached the exit gate, where her friends were now gathered, she was screaming like a siren herself.

Chapter 5

The three of them huddled round the rumpled copy of the Wakefield Express, as Tom read the paragraph aloud: "Local residents received more than the usual 'trick or treat' surprise on Friday, when a freak lightning strike destroyed a tomb in the heart of Raingate Cemetery…"

Doc interrupted, "Any mention of us lot?"

Tom closed the paper up. "Not a sausage. Lucky thing really," he said, raising his eyebrows and looking at Jazz, whose expression was difficult to read.

She bit off a chunk of her Mars Bar and nodded. "*Very* lucky," she mumbled through a mouthful of chocolate and caramel.

"Why?" Doc was slow to cotton on.

"Because," added Jazz, "If your parents sussed it out, they'd probably get a bit overprotective – and put the graveyard off limits."

The boys understood why Jazz hadn't included her own parents in that prediction; she was always going on about how much freedom her mum and dad allowed her – and that they'd buy her just about anything she wanted. Made the lads sick sometimes, that did. The strange thing was though, they hardly ever saw Jazz's parents.

The smell of recently-devoured pizza was still strong in the air as they sat silently for a while, except for Jazz's chomping. It was Tuesday and the night outside was cold and clear. Doc got up off his beanbag and, dodging dirty plates and the microphone stand, he drifted to the circular attic window. He could see for miles across the Wakefield skyline. The stars seemed to be winking at him as they danced playfully on the surface of Pugney's Water Park. This contrasted with the almost solid shadow of Sandal Castle's mound. The light and the dark…

Somehow this made him think of Jazz's howling exit from the cemetery after the lightning. Doc smiled and turned to his friends: "Would've been great to see your face though Jazz, if they'd splashed your antics all over the front page."

Tom burst out laughing. "Now, now, Doc – you know she doesn't like to be reminded of that!"

"Oh, do shut up," Jazz rolled her eyes.

"No, really," grinned Doc. "Those owls are terrifying. Particularly when they're scared more witless than you and flying harmlessly overhead!"

"Look!" Jazz jumped up, pointing a black-painted fingernail at Doc. "Either you ditch the owl gags – or you're going straight out the window." But she couldn't help smiling at his mischievous expression.

"But it's such a hoot!" Doc spluttered, as Jazz chased him round the attic, grabbed him and dumped him on a beanbag, like a sack of coal.

She's really strong – for a girl, thought Tom. Although they teased her about the screeching owl in the storm last Friday, they knew they'd all been pretty spooked by it. Only difference was that they'd been *outside* and she'd been on the inside, with the graves and the dead and who knows what else ..?

Now it was Jazz's turn to gaze out of the window: "Pretty weird though guys. Pretty weird…" They hadn't been to the graveyard since Halloween. There was still a stripy safety ribbon all the way round the crumbled remains of the tomb that had been struck by lightning; so kids were 'discouraged' from the area until further notice.

As she looked down at the scene, Jazz became lost in her thoughts. *Yes, there had been an owl that was startled that night. Yes, it had flown past the exit…*But Jazz knew that the terrible screeching sound she had heard – that had caused her to run in blind panic – had been no owl. No way. It had been something… *Something not normal.*

"Gotta go," announced Tom, as he and Doc slipped on their coats. Jazz saw them to the front door and waved them off; it was more than the cold November night that sent a shiver down her spine. The owl hooting in a distant tree seemed to be perfectly timed for chilling effect.

Jazz was all too aware that she still hadn't mentioned to anyone – not even Tom and Doc – about the awful stench that had invaded the graveyard that night. She had wracked her brains to try and place it, to identify it. She couldn't. The closest she could come to it was a mixture of stink bombs and sewage. A bit like when the workmen had opened the blocked drain outside school once. She was also keeping the necklace under wraps, for now – along with the nagging guilt that came with the taking of it. And something, deep inside her, made her unable to admit to *anyone* – let alone her friends – that she had been truly terrified that night. So she fronted it out. But the awful unease remained in her heart.

She glanced up, and the full bright moon sneered down at her. She turned quickly and slammed the night outside the door.

Chapter 6

Life goes on. School goes on. Trips to the swimming baths for Year 6 go on – and on … and on… Jazz hated the things; made a right mess of her hair. She was a good swimmer though – but she had learned her moves before the hair became an issue.

As the children disembarked – or perhaps *piled off* – the baths-bus, Doc gave Jazz a sly nudge from behind, "Way-hey! Say bye-bye to the hairspray, kid!" he chuckled. The half-playful tap on the shin with her back-heel, was enough to shut him up.

"Cool it kiddie-winkies," trilled Tom, in a very poor imitation of Miss Lidley, the Headmistress. Smiling, Jazz did a mock flick of her spiked hair-do, which wouldn't have moved even in a force 10 gale, then headed into the big stone building that housed the pool.

"See you in there – R.I.P. hair," joked Doc, in one of his random rhymes, and skittered into the boys' changing room before Jazz could whack him with her bag. Tom followed, but not before giving Jazz a quick wave, which she briskly, but warmly returned.

The girls chattered noisily as they began to get ready, but Jazz locked herself into a cubicle to avoid the general clamour. As she began to unpack her swimming gear, she became newly-aware of the object in the pocket of her grey school trousers. Laying out her costume, and removing the strange necklace, Jazz let the glinting gold chain drape through her fingers, as the 'pendant' sat snugly in the palm of her hand.

She had never grown tired of looking at it, ever since finding it in the chaos of the graveyard on Halloween. The tang of guilt was constantly there, though, like a distant toothache; uncomfortable, but tolerable. They had made a pact that they would never take anything from the graveyard playground; it would be kind of like stealing from the dead.

But this… this had been different. It had *drawn* Jazz to it. It still drew her. Her eyes were slightly glazed, as she stared, fascinated, at the object attached to the end of the chain. It was yellowish, but not like the glimmering chain. It was *ancient* yellow; the colour that bone goes when it's really, really old. And the miniature skull *felt* like bone too. But Jazz knew that, logically, it couldn't really be a skull: it was no bigger than a thimble.

And yet…

As she looked into the darkness of its eye-sockets, Jazz felt that strange falling sensation again. As though she was being sucked into a black hole. She was a rabbit held in the hypnotic stare of headlights - but her mind was so detached that she didn't even realise it. Everything around her had ceased to exist. She was floating in deep, dark space, with only the necklace to guide her.

Bang – bang – bang! "Come *along* Jasmine!" The dulcet tones of Miss Robshaw jolted her from her dream state.

"Coming, Miss!" Jazz chimed back, blinking hard and tossing the necklace onto her towel, as the 'skull' suddenly heated up, almost burning her hand.

But it couldn't have – could it?

Jazz inspected her hand but saw nothing unusual, no redness. No sign of a burn of any kind. But she had certainly felt the skull become hotter…

Rubbing her hands together rapidly she put the thought out of her mind. The necklace sat innocently on the rolled up towel. Jazz smiled at her own silliness and changed quickly, to catch the others up. Before leaving her cabin, she hooked the pendant around her neck and tucked it inside the front of her costume, hoping that Miss Robshaw wouldn't notice. It was still warm, but she figured the pool would cool it down – and she was unwilling to risk losing it to the changing room magpies!

Jazz stuffed her clothes into the nearest locker, keen to catch up with the rest of the class, before Miss Robshaw returned to roust her out. The changing room was empty, the last of the yattering girls having left a couple of minutes before. But… as she looked ahead to the end of the white-tiled room, Jazz saw a shadow…

To the left of the far wall was a recess that led into a small shower area, which then led into the pool area itself. She should be able to hear the normal sounds of a swimming pool from her position by the lockers – but she couldn't. She couldn't hear the teachers giving instructions, or the kids splashing. When she strained her ears, all that she detected was silence. Total silence.

Jazz took a step closer. The shadow moved; loomed nearer,

larger. It wasn't entirely shapeless; it had a kind of human form, but *different*. She could make out longer-than-natural fingers, with what seemed to be curving claws at the ends. And the head… The head had a life of its own! Jazz recalled seeing pictures of the Gorgon in their Ancient Greece history lessons, with its head of writhing snakes. But whilst this silhouette was similar, the head appeared to be on fire. She saw flames of black, twisting and stretching, reaching weirdly high from the large skull.

Jazz's heart began to do a double-time beat, as she now caught the first whiffs of the stinking-drain smell that she'd experienced in the graveyard that night.

She backed away, and the shadow shifted with her, the stench growing stronger. Jazz continued retreating until her back was pressed against the cold tiles of the wall, and she stopped still. But the shadow kept moving. The pendant began to feel hotter again, then the hideous shriek that she had been fearing to hear, rang out through the echoing changing room, like death's own scream:

"JASMINE BAXTER! *Get into that swimming pool at once!*"

Miss Robshaw loomed into view – and Jazz had never been so relieved to see her! She hurried past the teacher and into the pool area, where she dived into the water as eagerly as if she had been on fire.

As she surfaced amidst the other children, the water felt cool and healing; and the ominous feeling that had gripped her back in the changing room, lifted from her shoulders and seemed to evaporate into the atmosphere.

Tom looked over at her and she grinned. But – Tom noticed – the grin didn't reach her eyes; something else lingered there.

Something like fear.

Chapter 7

"There you go, milk and chocolate muffins."

"Thanks a lot, Mrs Allerton." Doc loved going to Tom's house. "Home-baked, as usual?"

"Oh yes, dear. Fresh out of the oven an hour ago," smiled Tom's mum.

Tom and Doc were enjoying the snack, before heading off to Jazz's for a rehearsal; Doc always made sure he got to Tom's well-early, so as not to miss out on the treats – Mrs Allerton had a bit of a soft spot for him.

"Thanks Mum," said Tom, as his mother left the front room, heading back to the bubbling pan of stew that would be the evening meal for her and Tom's dad, Ted.

Calling back over her shoulder, she gently warned: "Mind you don't go spoiling your tea though." Tom and Doc grinned at each other through crumby lips. The fire crackled reassuringly in the grate and the boys felt cosy and warm.

"Yep," Doc agreed, "Need to save some room for the hotdogs at Jazz's."

"Mmm…" munched Tom. "Been working on a new song. Might try it at rehearsals tonight."

Doc groaned. "Zombies again?"

"Nope." A mysterious look passed over Tom's face, as he whispered, "*Graveyard Explosion*'s the working title."

"Nice one. Did you talk to Jazz for inspiration?"

"Tried to – but she didn't say much." A sort of *distant* expression came into Tom's eyes, and he stared into the flickering flames. His voice had quietened slightly when he next spoke. "Got the impression she was holding something back; wasn't telling me everything about that night…" His focus shifted as his eyes roved up to the mantelpiece, finally resting on the photo of his dad, in his fireman's uniform – yellow helmet tucked under his arm.

"Like what?" Doc startled him back to the here and now.

"Huh? Dunno. Just… can't put my finger on it, you know?" Tom drained his milk, as if to dismiss the thought, then stuffed the last of his muffin into his mouth. "Come on," he crumbled, patting Doc's leg.

"Wait up!" Doc grabbed the remains of his double-choc-chip and, following brief goodbyes to Tom's mum, they pulled on their coats and went out into the cool evening air, heading for Jazz's place.

Tom was still deep in thought, as they arrived and knocked on Jazz's front door.

Chapter 8

They took a break. The rehearsal was going even more slowly than normal; Tom's *Graveyard Explosion* idea had caused Jazz to lose concentration. Hotdogs were consumed and washed down with Dandelion 'n' Burdock.

Jazz was gazing out of the big round window that looked across the graveyard. They'd taken the stripy plastic barriers away now; obviously the council believed there was no more danger to the public – or inquisitive kids.

"You alright?" Tom was genuinely concerned for Jazz, who just carried on staring out into the night, lost in thought.

The boys exchanged glances, and Doc touched Jazz's shoulder gently. "Hey, Jazz – y'okay?"

"What? Oh yeah, fine. Just a bit tired, that's all." She blinked her eyes rapidly, as if they stung, then stretched long and hard.

"Don't you like my song? Is that what's up?" Tom stuck his bottom lip out.

"Yep. Rubbish," Jazz smiled. "But that's not what's wrong; didn't sleep too good last night." She grabbed up her drum sticks and put them in her leather pouch.

The lads looked puzzled. "What about the rest of the rehearsal?" Doc enquired.

"I've had enough, guys. Bad headache." She turned and glanced out the window again, her back to the boys.

Tom silently nudged Doc and gestured to the door with his thumb.

"We'll be off then – mebbe see you tomorrow?" Tom tried to sound as light as possible.

"Sure," Jazz replied, without turning round.

As the boys got to the door, Doc placed his palm on the cool handle, then turned around. "Jazz?" he hesitated. "You would tell us if there was something wrong, wouldn't you?"

"Yeah, yeah," she piped, trying to sound more cheery than she felt. "Now, get outta here, you gruesome twosome!"

"'Kay," chorused the boys – and Doc pressed down on the cold metal handle, ready to push the door open.

That was when the smell hit their nostrils, all of a sudden, like a slap in the face from a rotting corpse's hand.

Chapter 9

Doc jerked his arm back from the handle. He hadn't opened the door –
not even by a crack – but the horrible smell of death and decay had
passed right through the solid wood. Both boys took a few steps back,
as if pushed by unseen hands; so strong was the feeling of dark menace
that accompanied the stink.

"Oh, *what's that?*" Tom retched, using his hands to cover his
mouth and nose.

Jazz had somehow appeared at both their sides. "Get back," she
warned.

"Jazz?" Doc looked alarmed. Impossibly, the smell grew
stronger; they felt like they could almost *chew* the hideous stuff.

Without looking round, Tom whispered: "Jazz, what *is* that?"
He was referring to the stench; but as he uttered the words, a wave of
black began to flood through, in the gap between the floor and the
bottom of the door. It looked like a tide of dark oil at first glance, but as
the three stared in horror, they could see that it was an army of scuttling
cockroaches that click-clacked as they infested the attic room.

Terror temporarily froze the children, as the seething black mass
washed around their feet. Then, as one, Tom, Doc *and* Jazz screamed
out loud, and Doc lunged for the door handle again, keen to get to the
stairs and escape this shuddering nightmare. He pushed downwards and

outwards – and the attic room door flew open to reveal the landing and the staircase that led steeply down to the two lower floors. Dim wall-lights illuminated the stairwell a little, casting shadows back, but only weakly.

It wasn't the shadows or the sheer drop down the deep, dark stairwell that caused the three friends to freeze again, as they tumbled out onto the landing, to the accompaniment of the squishing, popping sounds made by the crushed 'roaches beneath their feet. It was the hideous *thing* that faced them, on the opposite side of the banistered abyss; *that* and the two grotesque creatures that strained against leashes of steel chain, wrapped tightly around each of the monster's taloned hands.

Chapter 10

The temperature around the stairwell was astronomical; so hot that the children became instantly drenched in sweat. The heat made their eyes sting but they were still unable to drag their petrified stares from the horrors across the black drop.

A thing that resembled a woman *hovered* on the opposite landing. It was so skinny that it was almost skeletal, but the bone structure was covered with a tight, leathery skin; it looked like a floating corpse. A flowing dark-grey shroud billowed around its shimmering body, the hood of which concealed its head and face. Crisscrossed diagonally, from shoulders to waist, where they hooked into a bone-studded belt, were two lengths of a sort of rubbery-rope material; like a weird pair of braces. Dangling from these, like charms on nightmare bracelets, were masses of misshapen objects. Tom had to screw up his eyes to make out what they were, then – awfully – it dawned on him. They were a collection of *shrunken heads.* Some were just bone; some had shreds of manky-looking skin clinging to them. *All* had dark, empty, staring eye sockets, and their jaws hung limply.

Tom thought they looked like they were screaming with the sound turned down.

With the chain still firmly in its grasp, the creature raised a hand, and drew back the hood. The monster's head was the weirdest of all. It was long and thin – and evil.   Arching nostrils flared over a wide gash of a mouth that was filled with needle-sharp fangs. Deep-set black eye sockets disappeared into the skull, each punctuated only by a red pinpoint of light, bright as lasers. But the *hair.* It wasn't really hair. The kids couldn't make sense of it; it looked like the head was on *fire.* Where the hair should have been, flames leapt and crackled from the skull, in colours of red, blue, orange and yellow. Choking white coils of smoke twisted and wound themselves like unearthly snakes around the hissing, salivating head. It was now frighteningly clear where the burning heat came from.

The beast-bodyguards resembled giant scorpions; black, armour-plated, lethal-looking, with snapping front claws and curved-over tails pointing payloads of poison straight at the terrified trio. Worst of all, each one had a weirdly-human face that looked as if it had been stuck on by some escaped lunatic. Their eyes glowered and their lips curled back to reveal discoloured and gappy teeth.

And the *stink* and *heat* grew stronger with every rattling heartbeat.

The thirty foot drop that formed the space across the stairwell didn't feel like much protection to them, particularly as the monster was hovering in midair! Her 'guards' though, were reassuringly in contact with the floor.

The children were speechless. They didn't even look at each other - their eyes were riveted on the seemingly alien creatures.

The sweat that soaked their bodies was not just down to the

unnatural heat; it was also due to the fear that gripped them all. Tom tried to swallow but his throat was too dry; Doc tried to yell, but his mouth was parched.

The monster-woman hissed across at them, hot spit flying from her gashy mouth. Her graveyard-rotten breath came at them like a ghastly hair drier, making the stench on the landing so bad that Jazz felt like throwing up. She probably would have too, except something distracted her: her lower neck area felt as if it were being pressed by red hot branding irons.

To her terror, she realized this was the precise place on her body where the stolen pendant nestled. At the precise moment that this dawned on Jazz, the she-monster nodded her head and, eyes blazing with evil, unleashed a hideous screech – the sound of a thousand attacking bats! The scorpion bodyguards growled like rabid dogs.

Jazz clenched her teeth against the sizzling pain of the necklace and took a step backwards, with retreat firmly in mind. She may as well have pulled the creature's trigger! The corpse-like thing launched herself straight at Jazz.

Three things happened very quickly. The friends found their voices and screamed; the monster flew like a rocket over the deep stairwell; and the scorpion guards nearly had their necks pulled off as their chains yanked them straight after their mistress!

Within the beat of a humming bird's wings, the she-monster had crossed the steep drop of the stairs and, talons outstretched, was within millimetres of clawing the soft flesh of Jazz's throat.

Then the monster stopped. It just stopped. For a fraction of a second, which felt like much longer, as time seemed to have temporarily gone into extra slow-motion, the skeletal beast just stayed put, in mid-air. The rasping sound of metal on wood revealed the cause of this delay; the chains of the guard-beasts had become snagged on the banister rail. Hope rose briefly in the children's hearts, as the monster twisted and jolted – caught fast by her own leashes.

The relief, however, was short-lived, as the woman-thing became more enraged than ever, and her fiery hair flared into a towering inferno that threatened to incinerate the whole house and everything in it.

The unbearable heat made the children close their eyes. Their eyeballs felt as if they were melting.

A new sound came into the chaos now; a different kind of hissing, that sounded similar to a shower. The entire place instantly cooled as water cascaded down on the whole weird scene.

Jazz was first to open her eyes and, looking up, she quickly realized what had happened. The sprinkler system in the ceiling had been activated by the flames and now everything was getting drenched by glorious cool water.

With a look of excruciating pain on her bony face, the monster let loose one last howling screech, and disappeared – literally – in a huge puff of smoke, along with her toxic guardians.

Doc sank to his knees and Tom leaned forward onto the banister rail. They both looked at Jazz, as if she had some kind of answer to this madness. Somewhere, nagging at the back of both boys' minds, was the suspicion that she knew more than she was letting on.

Jazz didn't return their look. She just stood, dumb-struck, fingering something that hung around her neck. It looked like it was bothering her – like a very bad itch that she just couldn't scratch.

Chapter 11

It's a safe bet that when people get mortally threatened by a weird flying monster attached to two gigantic scorpions, it's going to leave an impression. And it did. Jazz, Tom and Doc were three kids who had experienced a life-changing event – and that needed talking through! BUT – parents were parents too; and even Jazz's parents had gone crazy when they returned home about half an hour after the sprinklers had smoked the monsters in the stairwell.

They'd been out to a posh restaurant on 'corporate' business, as they called it. Basically, that meant they were buying dinner for some rich businessman and trying to get him to invest in some of their property developments. That's what Jazz's mum and dad were into – 'property development'. And it took up much of their time, leaving Jazz to her own devices a lot. When Tom's dad was a bit tired one night, Tom overheard him say to his mum that Mr and Mrs Baxter had more time for their business than they did for Jasmine. But, Tom thought, it would be really cool to have as much freedom as she had, at least sometimes.

Jazz's parents had arrived home in posh frock and tuxedo to find the three children on their hands and knees with a bucket, wringing out clothfuls of water, from their precious carpet. And the place smelt like it had been on fire!

The children had a choice to make: either they told the truth (flappy, flame-headed floaty woman with extra-large scorpion bodyguards…) or they made something up that might sound a bit more plausible.

Jazz took the decision quickly when she saw her mum's mega-cross expression.

"Sorry, Mum. Sorry, Dad. We were smoking – and the sprinklers went off."

Smoking! The boys were so gobsmacked you could have knocked them *down* with a cigarette! Jazz looked at them with a silent apology and a shrug that suggested it was all she could think of. Mrs Baxter very quietly - and it was all the more worrying because of that - asked the boys to leave. That night, neither Tom nor Doc slept very well, always expecting the Baxters to call their parents with the bad news.

Those calls never came, much to their surprise. Jazz got grounded for a week - but they let her off after one day! In the end, the three friends got their first chance to discuss the strange happenings when they were at school the following day. They'd eaten lunch and the weather was pouring down outside, so it was a wet break. Miss Robshaw was sitting at her desk, ploughing through a pile of marking, and various clusters of kids were playing board games or drawing pictures or making Lego masterpieces. Jazz and Co were on the beanbags in the book corner, pretending to share a book, trying to divert any attention from themselves. The overactive spider plant on top of the book shelf was tickling the top of Tom's head as the boys sat in silence, looking intently at Jazz. If there had been one time in her life that she wished the ground would open up and swallow her, this was it. After what seemed like an eternity, she managed to raise her eyes and look at them. She cleared her throat and said quietly: "Guys – there's something I need to tell you about."

"Well, HOO-ray," Doc muttered impatiently, continuing to stare at her.

Tom put his hand on Doc's arm to stop him. "No, Doc. Let her carry on." Doc sighed deeply – for effect – but said nothing more.

Jazz took a deep breath. "Well… It's like this… I think I might have an idea what was behind all that stuff at my house. I'm really sorry, but I – "

At this point a huge tower of Lego bricks, that was supposed to be a spaceship, crashed over and various colours and sizes of bricks pinged, clattered and bounced towards the book corner; one even hitting Jazz on the nose.

"Be careful, numbskull!" Jazz yelled.

"Jasmine Baxter, apologise at once – it was only an accident!" Miss Robshaw's decisive voice boomed across the classroom.

"Sorry," Jazz mumbled.

"Apology accepted," grinned Jamie Rankin, the spaceship designer. "Keep yer 'air on," he added in a whisper, winking at Jazz. Jazz only managed a weak smile. This little distraction did not get her off the hook. As soon as Jamie had gathered up his shattered bits of spacecraft, Tom urged her on again. "Go on, Jazz. What on earth was all that about? I didn't sleep a wink last night."

Jazz proceeded to get the whole thing off her chest. She confessed to breaking the gang's golden rule – taking the necklace from the graveyard; she described the weird feeling she had experienced when she'd gazed into the tomb, as though she was being pulled into another world; she explained about the strange happening in the swimming pool changing rooms; and she told the boys that she knew why the monster-woman went straight for her throat last night… it was for the necklace.

There was a pause before Doc asked, in a surprisingly gentle voice, "Why didn't you tell us, Jazz?"

She examined the swirly pattern on the book corner's blue carpet again, her shoulders slumped. "I dunno. I felt bad for taking it in the first place… you know, with our rule and everything."

"Well, why don't we just go and put it back?" Tom suggested.

"Whoa, whoa, wait a minute." Doc's finger was up in the air and this was always a sign – a bad sign – that he was having a 'bright idea'. "Listen," Doc continued, "If this thing, this *necklace*, has stirred up such a bunch of weirdness, then maybe it has some kind of power. *Maybe*… we could make some money out of it; enough to cover the cost of our first CD?" he beamed.

"I'm not sure I like where you're going with this," warned Jazz.

"Look," Doc persisted. "We can't undo the past; you've nicked he necklace, and that's that." His bluntness hit Jazz like a cold wet kipper. "But at least we can try and find a positive side."

"Can we see it?" asked Tom.

Jazz fumbled inside her collar and lifted the pendant over her head, careful - even now – not to mess up her painstakingly plumed hair. She handed the necklace to Tom, but it was Doc who spoke: "Wow, it's a little yellow skull…"

"Keep your voice down," hissed Tom, as space-commander Rankin glanced across, then returned his attention to rebuilding his Lego starship.

"D'you think it's a real head?" Doc said, more quietly.

"Well – *d'urrh!* - " mocked Jazz. "Look at the *size* of it. Do you see many heads the size of a sprout?"

"No. A few brains, though," he retorted, looking over the top of his specs in a professorly way.

"Point taken," she surrendered.

Tom interjected. "I think we should take it back. Can't risk any more of the stuff from last night."

Jazz nodded slowly – but Doc came in quickly: "Okay, but at least let my dad check it out first. He might be able to tell us how old it is, and whether it's real bone or not."

Tom and Jazz looked uncertain, but Doc was on a roll. "Aren't you just a *bit* curious? I mean, imagine us never, *ever*, knowing what it is – 'specially after all that's happened. It'd probably drive us all mad, and we would die gibbering in a mental home!"

Tom and Jazz had to smile: Doc was such a drama-queen at

times. But he could see they were weakening. "Come on," he wheedled. "I could give it to him tonight, to check out at work tomorrow." Doc's dad's job at Leeds University was in the Archaeology Department, and his specialist equipment would have answers in no time.

"Just one night?" Jazz said slowly, though Tom still didn't commit.

"One night," Doc confirmed. "Then Dad'll give it back to me tomorrow when he gets home – and it can have a decent burial back in the graveyard."

"Tom?" Jazz looked at him for a decision.

He exhaled slowly, wringing his hands thoughtfully. "Okay," he said. "One night."

"*Yes!*" Doc whisper-shouted, and his friends shushed him again, as Interstellar Rankin looked up at them. "Alright?" Doc winked at him. "I think it's toppling again." And at this, Jamie Rankin returned urgently once more to his space creation.

Doc wrapped the necklace in his - mercifully clean - hanky, and pushed it deep into his pocket, before Jazz added ominously: "Oh – and one more thing – if you feel it starting to get hot, start to panic."

"Why?" Doc stretched the word out, a puzzled look on his face.

"Because," Jazz spoke in a hush, "that's when all Hell breaks loose."

Chapter 12

The following evening, Doc was stretched out on his belly, propped on his elbows, peering intently out of his bedroom window. He was scanning the street like a hawk, watching out for Dad's silver Zafira to come cruising round the corner. He'd done his homework ages ago and Mum was used to him disappearing off to play in his room, if he wasn't out with Tom Allerton and Jasmine Baxter.

He could smell the lovely aroma of Spaghetti Bolognese wafting up the stairs from the kitchen below; that was his and Dad's favourite. He looked forward to the conversation over tea tonight, when Dad would reveal what the pendant was actually made out of. Doc's dad was great; he'd been only too willing to take the mystery item into the University to run some tests on it. Said it would help keep his detective brain sharp!

Mrs Rattenbury, the nice old lady from next-door-but-one, was returning from the corner shop with a small plastic carrier bag. Probably cat food for Marmalade, her ancient ginger tomcat (Doc figured the cat was definitely older than him, and probably not far off Mrs Rattenbury too!)

The late-autumn light was starting to fade, when he heard that deliciously familiar sound that he knew was Dad's car engine. Piercing headlights signalled the arrival of Dad, and Doc rolled from his bed, commando-style, crushing his latest Dr Who magazine in the process! He scrambled to his feet and took the stairs two at a time, thumping noisily in his haste to get to the front door.

"Hey – Mr Heffelump! Take it easy, will you?" shouted Mum, light-heartedly.

"Sorry!" Doc responded with a giggle. He unlatched the front door and opened it before Dad had even pulled the car into the drive. As Dad drew the car to a halt and turned off the engine, Doc had pattered out in his bare feet and yanked open the driver-door for him.

"Hi Dad!" he grinned, expectantly.

"Well, hello," said Dad, pushing up his glasses with an index finger. "What's this – after extra pocket money?"

"No Dad! Come on, tell me: what did you find out about the necklace?" he pleaded, eyes wide and expectant behind smudged lenses.

But Dad didn't respond with his usual easy smile and tease. Instead, he opened his mouth to speak, then seemed to think better of it and closed his lips again, staring into space.

"Dad? Come *on!* What's the news?"

Dad unwound himself from the car and shut the door behind him. He placed a hand on Doc's shoulder, whilst with the other he thumbed the central locking button on his car key. "Danny," he said, his face serious, "I ran every test imaginable on that thing today- "

"And?" Doc urged him on, relentlessly.

"*And,*" Dad continued with a long exhalation, "The materials on that pendant were not recognised by any of the analyses that I put them through."

Dark clouds had gathered overhead, as if huddling in to listen, and a chill breeze stroked the back of Doc's neck like the fingers of a ghost. "But I thought you had all the top range stuff at the Uni. How come it didn't work?" Doc's voice oozed disappointment.

"Oh, there's nothing wrong with the machines," Dad began to shepherd Doc towards the open front door, as drops of icy rain began to splat down. "But what that *does* mean is that you've got quite a find there. Whatever the necklace is made out of appears to be material that has never been discovered before."

"What? *Never?*" Doc was taken aback; even after all that he'd seen recently, he'd expected Dad to come up with at least *something*.

"Well..." Dad smiled, in an attempt at reassurance, "At least, never on *this* planet. Come on, let's get inside."

Doc's stomach did a somersault, as he stepped through the front door; and thunder grumbled somewhere high in the leaden sky.

Chapter 13

Doc woke very early the next morning, after another uneasy night of fitful sleep. He couldn't tell whether he was excited, nervous, plain-scared – or a mixture of all three. Dad had told him that he wanted to hold on to the necklace for another day, so that he could repeat the tests and, if that concluded nothing, then he would consult his old friend, Professor Creswell, who was now an independent consultant on "antiques, curios and obscurities", whatever they were… Doc had reluctantly agreed, knowing that he had promised to return the necklace that very day.

Deep thinking and moral dilemmas had disturbed his sleep. Should he keep his word to Dad and break his oath to Jazz and Tom? Or should he betray Dad's trust and take the necklace back to his friends, to tell them of the very real possibility that it was from another planet?

He had made his decision well before rising that morning. He thanked Mum through a mouthful of toast, as he grabbed his school bag and coat – and was out of the door before she could even tell him to finish his drink. The slamming of the front door caused Dad to jump whilst brushing his teeth: he was usually the first to leave for work. He opened the bathroom window, to see Doc disappearing off up the street. *Early for school?* He put two and two together quickly and, rinsing his mouth, he hurried to his study to check his bottom desk drawer.

His heart felt a little heavy as he stared at the empty space where the pendant had been.

Chapter 14

The chill wind tugged persistently at them. Doc had called for Tom first, as was their routine, and then they had collected Jazz. As they passed by the cemetery they all glanced in, but no one voiced their inner thoughts. They made their way in silence through the stretch of woods that was their short-cut to school, as Tom and Jazz mulled over the news about the strange necklace. Big decisions had to be made; they knew that much, and had agreed to meet in the attic that night over at Jazz's place.

The bare branches of the trees wagged accusing fingers above their heads. The spectre of Sandal Castle loomed large, its ruined battlements rising jaggedly from the bailey like the shattered bones of a dead ogre. Hereabouts, the history books told that the rivers once ran red with blood from the soldiers of the clashing armies in the Battle of Wakefield. Doc shuddered as the thought flickered across his mind and, on this occasion, wished that he didn't read so much...

The rain from the thunderstorm last night had now stopped, though the ground was soft, and black clouds scudded across the sullen sky, threatening to pour down any time soon.

Tom's private thoughts didn't help his peace of mind. All of a sudden, life had become unexpectedly complicated. Just days ago, football and rock music were the main things in his mind. Now he had a dilemma. It was exciting in many ways: they could make history with this find; they could make the headlines; they could make lots and lots of money.

And yet... there was danger – right here, right now in his life. Real danger, life-threatening and alien. Things were getting out of control, yet he still had the loyalty to his best friends to consider. He wanted to talk it over with Dad, but he didn't know how to begin. He felt torn between the two. Perhaps Dad would be able to offer some help. But how? He'd always helped Tom before with his problems, but this was different: Tom felt he had glimpsed another world, and he was afraid that Dad might not understand, and that involving him might even put Dad in danger. He felt hot and uncomfortable, despite the cold temperature of the morning, and he knew that this was what confusion and guilt felt like.

The palpable silence between the children was punctuated only by the conspiratorial whispering of the wind in the spindly trees and their trudging feet.

Sweat trickled down Tom's back and, as he glanced towards Jazz, he noticed that she, too, was perspiring. Doc also had a troubled expression and was hurriedly slackening his tie. Tom gagged as the awful smell hit his nostrils and, as he looked ahead to the edge of the woods a hundred metres in front, he could barely understand what he saw. The perimeter trees were sending plumes of grey up into the cold morning air. They gave the impression of a cluster of skeletons exhaling clouds of hot breath, or a group of old men with gnarled bodies emitting fogs of smoky breath…

The three friends shared a common feeling of terrible fear at this sight. As Tom watched on, the very fabric of time warped and slowed for his eyes. The smoke now rose lazily, in slow-motion towards the beckoning sky. It thickened, like a smoggy curtain, gradually and unhurriedly eclipsing the trees. Tom's eyes stung and they would have watered if only they hadn't been so dry. He was so transfixed that he couldn't even blink and was completely unaware of anything or anyone except for the shield of smoke. Nevertheless, *something* was moving within the depths of the murk. This thing, whatever it was, began to take shape as it emerged from the camouflaging fog. It was like a frame by frame slowed-down film; but all too soon, the grim realization dawned on Tom that he had seen this creature before. Grinning, or leering, with wicked needle teeth, the monster hovered – just as it had in the attic, three nights ago. Then the fluttering ghostly form inhaled very deeply, its chest inflating like a barrel. The tiny points of light in its black eyes blazed now, as it screeched long and high. The children lifted their hands to cover their ears but the gestures were futile against the demonic scream. They fell to their knees, resigned to the probability that this was the end; the alien creature would not stop until they were scramble-brained and dead.

Unexpectedly, and to the immense relief of the children, the screeching *did* stop. Quite suddenly. Then the monster blew out its ragged lips and projected a large quantity of something luminous-green and thickly-liquid. The substance hurtled through the air, a weird globular cloud of green muck, in the same ultra-slow fashion. It landed on Doc's hand with a sickening, stinky, enveloping squelch: sticking it, like fast-drying glue, to the tree stump on which it rested.

Frozen with terror, Jazz and Tom looked in disbelief at Doc's trapped hand.

That was the moment that the pace of time restored itself to normal. The smoke blossomed rapidly, like a dark grey ghoul. The creature rose up higher and its flailing hair erupted once more into blazing flames. The chains around its leathery wrists jangled and from out of the thick smog scuttled the frighteningly-familiar giant scorpion-guards. They clacked and smacked their huge claws and whipped their poisonous tails in anticipation of the massacre to come. Malicious grins spread across their oddly-human faces.

Thunder boomed right on dramatic cue, as the monster began to drift towards them with a cruel smile twisted onto her grotesque face. The heat was almost unbearable, the stench made breathing nigh-on impossible, and the glue-like green substance had now solidified, holding Doc prisoner. Now trees all around them in the wood were flaring up in orangey-yellow crackling flames.

As the necklace scorched his thigh through his trouser pocket, and he tugged in vain at his green-glued hand, Doc had the awful feeling that they had all strayed into Hell.

Lightning cracked the dismal sky like a yellow scar and the clouds burst violently, sending torrents of icy rain down with startling speed. Stark contrasts of fire and icy water overwhelmed the senses of the young friends and with their minds full of swirling chaos, they slid into unconsciousness - like spiders down plugholes - with the mad, gleeful laughter of the she-creature and the snap-clattering of her guards ringing in their ears.

Chapter 15

Tom awoke to the feeling that he was being blasted by a high pressure hose. His vision was blurry and his whole body ached. His head swam dizzily. He was lying face down in slick mud, and a sickly smell assaulted his nostrils.

Disorientated at first, vivid memories of what had happened in the woods soon flooded back to Tom's brain. He staggered to his feet, his stomach lurching as he did so. He knew what was coming and he stumbled to a nearby bush to be sick. Tom remained bending forward until the nausea passed. He didn't know it, but he was suffering from the after-effects of shock; awful images of flaming trees and smoking ghouls filled his head.

"Aw, yuk!" Doc startled him from his thoughts and he was grateful for that. Tom straightened and turned to see Doc attempting to shake green glop from his hand, leaping round like a mad ostrich. It dawned on Tom that it was the green gunk that stank so badly.

Jazz – where was Jazz?

Casting his eyes around, Tom soon spotted her. Jazz was standing a few metres away, leaning on a tree whose branches wept in the still-fierce rainstorm. Her eyes were red-rimmed, and Tom knew she'd been crying.

Doc continued waving his hand like a mad traffic policeman.

Tom looked again at Jazz. Her eyes flicked up and met his own; a single tear trickled down her cheek, becoming lost in the streaks of rain. Without even thinking, Tom squelched over to Jazz, put his arms round her, and gave her a massive hug. In normal circumstances she would have most likely attempted to strangle him for this but, though she made no sound, Tom felt her body shuddering, and was all too aware that she was sobbing on his shoulder.

"Yes! *Yes!*" Doc broke the moment with his whooping. Jazz and Tom (rather self-consciously) parted and turned to see him, Jazz hurriedly wiping her eyes with the heels of her hands.

"Look! It's coming off!" Doc was referring to the green slime, which now seemed to be dissolving and was disappearing into the cloddy, churned-up earth at their feet. Doc looked angry and victorious at the same time, as the last of the weird green stuff drained away into the ground.

"Where did that stuff come from? What *was* it?" Jazz whispered, shaking with the wet and the cold.

Doc had no reply. As his mind flicked back to the surreal events that had happened, he had an inkling to the answer. But as he looked around, soggy and exhausted, at the innocent trees and the driving rain, Doc had difficulty convincing himself that any of this had actually happened.

Chapter 16

The day at school had seemed interminable. Soaked and bedraggled, they'd arrived at their classroom to find that Mr Wilton, the other Year 6 teacher, was looking after both classes. Somehow, even after the hair-raising incident in the woods, they'd only been ten minutes late. Mr Wilton gave them some PE kit to change into, until their stuff dried on the radiators, and they muddled through. Miss Robshaw was delayed because the unusually heavy downpour had caused chaos on the M62. She eventually *did* arrive - at around 10:30 - and had remained in a foul mood all day.

As Doc sat now on his bed, opposite Dad, who was seated on a stool, he was lost in his own recollections of the ambush earlier in the day. In all his eleven years, he had never come across anything that could have prepared him for how to react in a situation like that; deep down, he knew that he could live to a thousand and not know how.

In the end, he and Jazz and Tom had spent very little time making a decision; they wanted an end to all this. They agreed to meet in the attic at Jazz's house that very night at 6:30.

Doc glanced at his bedside clock and wrung his hands together – 5:20. Tea had mostly been an uncomfortable silence, then Dad had said he wanted to talk to Doc.

"Well, Daniel?" Dad leaned forward, looking earnestly into

Doc's eyes, which were downcast. He put his hand under his son's chin, gently lifting his head, so that he had no option but to look at Dad. Dad detected the near-to-tears look in Doc's eyes and, though he continued, he did so gently. "Daniel?" he quietly repeated.

Doc really didn't know how to broach the subject. He reached into his pocket and took out the necklace. "Dad. I'm really sorry for taking this without telling you." Dad reached out for the necklace, but Doc closed his fist around it. "But," he added, "There was some stuff I didn't tell you about."

Dad sat back and placed his hands in his lap.

Doc maintained eye-contact. "I know I should have told you, Dad, but I'd made a promise to Jazz and Tom…"

Dad nodded slowly, encouraging him to carry on.

"I'd made a deal to bring it back the next day – that was today."

Dad spread his hands, a look of puzzlement on his face, "If that's so, Daniel, why do you still have it now?"

Davros, Doc's goldfish, plopped up out of his water, then back into the bowl with a splash. That was Davros' weird habit; his 'party piece', Dad called it. Somehow, this little incident triggered a rush of remorse through Doc; he hated the feeling that he had let Dad down. He took a deep breath, his eyes moist and red. "Dad… It's just some stuff that's been going on with me and my mates."

"Tom and Jasmine?" Dad prompted.

"Yes. We've had a really bad day today…"

Dad reached out and put his hand on Doc's shoulder. "Have you fallen out?"

"No, nothing like that, Dad." He sniffed and looked at the gathering darkness outside his window. The halogen street lamp looked like a fiery eye, full of threat. He averted his gaze and looked down at the carpet. How could he explain this weird situation to Dad? If he did, Dad would never let him out tonight; but he just couldn't lie to him – he and Dad were too close for that.

"So – what then?" Dad tilted his head to one side, his manner gentle, his tone kind and patient.

Perhaps, if he told Dad *some* of the problem, but not all, then that wouldn't exactly be lying, would it? It would just be leaving chunks out... "We got soaked, Dad, and Miss Robshaw was late because the motorway was jammed up."

"Mm-hmm," Dad intoned.

"So I didn't get chance to speak to Jazz and Tom much. I need to see them tonight to sort it out, once and for all."

Dad stood up and walked to the work-station in the corner of Doc's bedroom. He clicked on the lamp, and turned back to Doc, his figure silhouetted like a ghost's. "Daniel, haven't you told them about my findings at work yesterday? That the materials on that thing are not even recognized?"

Doc shook his head, leaning forward and putting his hands behind his neck. "No. Like I said, we didn't get chance. Please, Dad – I need to see them tonight, to tell them."

Dad turned, so that he was standing facing the window.

59

Eventually, he spoke: "You know, Daniel, I would hope that if there was anything else on your mind, you would feel able to tell me about it." He didn't add anything more; just stood there, gazing out of the window.

The silence was broken only by the occasional splish from Davros.

The digits on the clock flickered to 5:42.

After what seemed like an age, Doc put the necklace back in his pocket, got up, and went over to stand by Dad. He put his arm round Dad's waist. "Dad… Just trust me, please. I need to work this one out myself. But I promise, I'll tell them what you found out at the Uni – and I'll bring the necklace back tonight."

He couldn't think of anything else to say. He refused to tell a lie to Dad.

He waited, tensely.

Then he felt the reassuring touch of Dad's arm wrapping round his shoulder, and pulling him in tight.

Father and son stood looking out into the approaching night.

The cloudless sky looked cold – and the stars appeared sharp, like thorns in dark flesh.

Chapter 17

In the end, Doc's dad had agreed to a compromise. The group was allowed to meet, but Doc had had to call his friends, to rearrange the meeting at *his* house. When Tom and Jazz had passed Mr and Mrs Studd in the hallway, they had uttered very brief but polite 'hellos' and avoided eye-contact as much as possible. Doc had been on hand to rescue them from too much embarrassment, and he whisked them off upstairs to his room for the conflab.

The boys were seated on the edge of Doc's bed, whilst Jazz perched on a comfy chair, which was adorned with a Cyberman print. Posters of Daleks, Stone Angels and even the occasional Judoon peered out menacingly from the walls, but the children were fully focused on the very real issues of fiery monsters and giant scorpions.

The atmosphere in the room was unusually subdued, and Tom spoke very quietly as he said, "Doc – this has all gone too far. It's got well out of hand."

A light tap at the door was followed by the entry of Mum, with orange juice and biscuits on a tray. "Hope I'm not interrupting," she trilled, but Doc knew by the way that her voice went 'up' at the end of the sentence that she was not altogether happy. He also knew that, whatever happened, it would not be the last he heard of this.

"Thanks Mrs Studd," Tom and Jazz chimed together, but they

didn't feel at all as comfortable as they tried to sound.

As Doc's mum exited the room, she left the door slightly ajar, but Doc rose and, rather guiltily, clicked it shut. His shoulders sagged as he heard his mother sigh loudly from the other side, then descend the stairs with heavy footfalls.

Doc didn't sit back down, bur wandered over to Davros, flicking open the lid on his tub of fish food. He looked troubled as he sprinkled a couple of pinches onto the surface of the water; Davros, however, just looked focused on gobbling as much and as fast as he could. The popping and splooshing noises he made were the only sounds that broke the silence in the room.

"It has to go back, you know." Jazz was emphatic when she spoke.

Doc clicked the fish food closed, staring blankly at the lid.

"Doc?" It was Tom. "Doc, we have to get this sorted out."

The silence that followed was as solid and as sharp as the edge of a knife. Muffled voices could be heard from downstairs; Doc's parents sounded troubled.

Eventually, Doc replaced the fish food on the table and turned to face his friends. "I promised Dad that I wouldn't take the pendant today. But I did. I think it's the first time I've ever properly lied to him." His voice was flat, fed-up.

"These are very unusual circumstances, Doc. I reckon you can be forgiven just this once, mate."

Doc appreciated Tom's kind words, but somehow it didn't

really lift that awful gnawing guilt that sat heavily in his heart. He crossed the room and sat once more on the bed, next to Tom. "I still haven't told him what's been going on and... I haven't told you guys yet why Dad needs to take the necklace back for more tests."

Three full glasses of orange juice and a plateful of chocolate biscuits remained untouched as Tom and Jazz listened, open-mouthed whilst Doc related what Dad had told him last night. Tom thought that the room, though brightly lit by Doc's bedside lamp - and a watching moon through the undraped window - dimmed slightly, as the news confirmed to them all what they already thought: the strange object really was from another world. And the things that were after it were alien too.

"Is your dad sure the machines were working properly? I mean, what if they were on the blink or something?" Jazz knew, even before she uttered these words, that she was clutching at straws. If the thing had been made out of any known material, the sophisticated equipment at the university would have picked it up. Even the wind, through the partially open window seemed to sigh in desperation.

"Jazz..." Tom found it hard to string his thoughts together. "Jazz – that thing is bad news. It's been bad news ever since you found it." New pangs of guilt surged through Jazz, like icy water, as she was reminded of her actions, and the dire consequences. Tom went on, "We know that all of this is straight out of a nightmare. Now, either that's all it is, and we'll all wake up in our beds soon, with the bad dream gone, or..."

Jazz finished for him, "Or we have to face up; we're being chased by an alien that wants to kill us."

"Or maybe it just wants that thing back," Tom nodded towards the necklace that Doc had removed from his pocket, and now had in the open palm of one hand.

"I can't," was Doc's short response. And now, his voice betrayed the tears that were on the brink of coming. Jazz, in particular, felt really uncomfortable about that; she'd never seen him that way. Now, Doc spoke through undisguised tears, "I can't put it back," he looked up quickly, to meet Tom's eyes, "not because I'm scared, but because I promised Dad." He rushed over to the window and opened it wide, feeling the welcome rush of cold air as he filled his lungs in a huge gulp.

Jazz started to rise from her chair but Tom was up first, and laid a gentle hand on her shoulder. She looked at him in surprise, and he slowly shook his head. Jazz took the hint, and Tom approached the window, where his friend was standing, staring out into the night. Tom didn't say anything – just stood by his side, looking into the same nightscape. The houses across the road were mostly lit up by now, people having returned home from work, normal lives being lived... As Tom considered this thought, he felt a bit envious; he felt that his 'normal' life had fallen to pieces. Now he was nagged by worries about life-threatening creatures from other worlds. The roofs of the town houses over the street were slickly black and glossy, like they had been newly varnished, following a short burst of rain earlier. Now the air was beautifully clean and cold. Beyond the houses, the lights of the town could be seen off to the left, whilst craggy old Sandal castle squatted, dark and sombre, away in the distance to the right. The moon looked down, liked the eye of a worried mother, whilst the stars threatened to gang up on the Earth.

Mr Ashworth, from number 22, pulled into his drive opposite. The black Mondeo shone darkly, even after he'd switched off the engine and killed the lights. He always looked very smart, and Doc supposed that was because he worked in the bank in town. Mr Ashworth's car bleeped twice and flashed orange, as the alarm was set, and his front door clicked softly to, behind him.

Tom risked a glance at Doc, not wanting to intrude, but knowing that they had to do *something*. Doc looked drained - empty. His eyes were staring out at the darkness, as if searching for an answer that wouldn't come.

"Doc. Y'okay?" Tom's words sparked no response from his friend. Doc still gazed out, like a sleepwalker. It was as if they'd all been photographed – Tom, Doc, Jazz, the unmoving night outside. Like a scene from a weird, frozen pantomime, where no one could remember the next line.

Then, Doc's face changed. His eyes suddenly sharpened again. An expression of surprise – shock? – and incomprehension came over him. Tom automatically looked across at the spot where Doc appeared to be gaping. There, bathed in the eerie yellow glow of the street lamp beneath Doc's window, stood a figure that gazed up at the boys. It was no ordinary figure: it looked ancient, a million years old. Yet its eyes burned with a brightness that only added to the weirdness of its shrivelled-brown skin and its long, wispy white hair. And those eyes bored into Tom and Doc, like twin beams that searched their souls.

The boys simultaneously looked at each other, as if each doubted his own sanity. The look of terror in the other's eyes confirmed to each that they *had* in fact seen this weird manifestation. When they glanced back down, the figure had gone.

And from behind them in the room, Jazz gave a scream of fear; a scream that became muffled, as something cut it short. The boys whirled around, and their blood ran cold as they saw the ancient, crinkled figure that had just been in the street below.

It had its hand over Jazz's mouth.

And it stared intently at them, with those oh-so sharp eyes, in that oh-so ravaged and crusty old face.

Chapter 18

Jazz's eyes were wide with fright. *What was it that had hold of her? Where had it come from?* She knew – for a fact – that only a second ago, there had only been her and the boys in the room. Yet now, she was being silenced by an unseen creature that had a gnarled old hand over her mouth! Except that it wasn't entirely unseen...

Jazz *could* see one of its arms. And from this she could tell that, at least, it wasn't the monster woman. The arm that she could see looked *prehistoric*. The skin on it was deeply scarred and furrowed. The muscles were strong and sinewy and caused the dark flesh to pull tight against their bulging size. In fact, the skin had split in places, to reveal shiny dark muscle structure underneath. It reminded Jazz of a crusty old mummy that she'd seen once in a museum, but more muscular. Its parchment coloured palm was outstretched and its blackened fingernails curled over slightly, giving the impression of blunt talons.

Great, thought Jazz grimly, *so I'm not going to be barbecued by the flying monster-girl, I'm going to be taken prisoner by Tutankhamun's great-grandad. Or worse... Why is it stretching out that huge old hand?*

She looked at the boys for answers, but they were just as baffled as she was. Tom and Doc peered at the unbidden stranger with feelings of dread. Unwelcome strangers were proving to be very dangerous for them just now. Their eyes flickered between the strangely reaching hand – it looked like it was waiting to be given change – and the face. It had a long, low forehead that sloped forward and downwards, forming a kind of canopy that overhung its deep-set eye sockets and searing eyes. The nose was bent and the nostrils flared. Its jutty-out jaw was covered by the same unkempt hair that draped over its head and shoulders. This hair theme continued all over its body, giving an impression of an old-aged werewolf crossed with a gorilla. None of this reassured either of them. The exact reason for the extended hand became very obvious in the next two seconds.

Davros decided to perform his party piece. The demented goldfish leapt gymnastically out of the water and straight over the side of the tank, in a spectacular loop-the-loop. Time seemed to wind down, like a slow-motion replay, as Davros started coming down, down, down - directly into the blistered palm of the figure across the room. Time returned to normal and the goldfish flipped and flopped in the massive hand.

What happened next surprised the children so much that the boys' jaws dropped open and Jazz's eyes nearly popped out of their sockets.

"If you promise to be quiet, I'll put the fish back in the water." The words had been spoken by the ancient giant, and before the children were able to answer, it had released Jazz and crossed the room to plop a very grateful Davros back into his tank.

Chapter 19

"Good, thank you," the hairy giant courteously said.

Now that they had had chance to scrutinize the figure more, the children could see that he was a *he,* not an *it.* He was the spitting image of a typical caveman. When he stood, his posture was slightly stooped, and that wasn't necessarily because of his squillion years; it was more to do with the fact that he resembled a cross between a big monkey and a very hairy man. Around his waist and looped over his shoulder, he wore some brownish-white animal skin, which definitely wasn't fake. Couple all this together with his bulging muscles and time-worn leathery skin, and the fact that he could actually speak, and it can be easily understood how the children were lost for words.

This just did *not* compute.

"Please, gentlemen, be seated." Tom and Doc did a quick scan around the room before they realised that he was, in fact, talking to them. The ancient one reinforced his words with a sweeping gesture of his hand – and the boys complied by crossing the bedroom to sit on the bed.

The children looked in bafflement at one another, with facial expressions that wordlessly said, "WHAT THE -?" But not one of them could operate their tongues. After all, what do you say when a real life caveman appears in your bedroom and rescues your goldfish?

"May I?" The caveman indicated that he wanted to sit on a stool by the window. The texture of his voice was like wet gravel. He sounded like a newsreader crossed with the guy who does the voice-overs for the movie-trailers at the cinema. Doc just nodded dumbly and rather slowly. Tom and Jazz didn't even move. Cavemen just weren't supposed to sound like that. As a matter of fact, they weren't supposed to talk at all. "Thank you," the old man said courteously.

"Y-you're welcome," Doc stammered, somehow finding his voice, and feeling surprised at how croaky it sounded. The irony of exchanging pleasantries with a prehistoric hunter-gatherer in the twenty-first century did not really dawn on Doc. "And thanks very much for saving Davros."

A confused expression flickered across the man's hairy features, then he smiled, showing blackened teeth, which hadn't seen a toothbrush in thousands of years. "Oh, the fish," he replied, glancing at the tank as the golden fins glistened in the moonlight. It was what the Caveman said next that gave the children a hint as to why he had materialized in this unusual place. "Although I am very pleased to have been able to save your little creature of the river, it is you that I have come to warn – to warn of very great and imminent danger."

So - it appeared that this massive prehistoric man had come to help!

It was as though he had read the thoughts of the children; sensed the glimmer of hope that his words may have given. He spoke in that gravelly-smooth voice of his, and his eyes scanned them all, "I fear that you have evoked an ancient evil; an evil that would have been best left buried…"

A chill wind started up outside, causing the curtains to billow and cast weird shadows around the room. It wasn't just the cold breeze from the open window that made the three friends shiver.

"You mean the monster woman, don't you?" Tom ventured, his voice uncertain.

"The very same," the ancient one replied.

Jazz leaned forward in her seat, her eyes searching the old one's eyes for some kind of hope, "Why are you here?" She hesitated before she added: "Are you able to help us?" The tone of her voice, and her whole manner, were different to anything that the boys had ever seen in her before. They were used to the hyper-confident, mad-haired drummer of their rock band; what they saw here was a totally vulnerable little girl, clutching at any thread of hope that might be available. She even *looked* small; but, perhaps anybody would, in the company of the ancient colossus that sat by the window.

The Caveman stared into space, as if lost in thought, or trying to dig out some long lost memory. Then he spoke. "Yes, I will try to help you."

Tom bit his lip to try to keep back the tears of relief that threatened to come.

"But how? How can you help? Are you going to have a fight with her or what? I mean, have you seen what she can do?" This was Doc; always the questioner.

"I have seen what she can do, yes," the Caveman gravelled, "And so have you. But you have seen only a fraction of what she is *capable of.* I have had many years – too many to count – to ponder the true nature of this being. Her evil is almost beyond understanding. She is not of this world; that much you already understand. But she is *ancient;* far, far older than me."

The children could not get their heads around that one; surely *nothing* could be older than a prehistoric cave man? They didn't voice their thoughts though, remaining hooked on his every word, as he continued. "In Earth terms, she is *billions* of years old. Her race, the Sweltian, have the gift of great, great longevity."

Jazz looked puzzled.

"They live for a very long time," Tom said, thinking he was being helpful.

"I knew that," Jazz retorted sharply.

Before the potential quarrel between the two of them was able to develop, the Caveman went on. "Yes – and she had lived for many years; but way, way out in space, in an entirely different solar system to this one. She was royalty, Princess Zeduza, but only second in line to the throne. Her older brother, Lakkesh, was to be crowned King, upon the death of their father." He paused, sucking in air to his vast lungs. Rain had started to fall lightly outside the window, creating a watery mist. "As I said, their race had longevity, but they were not immortal. King Queshna had but a short time of his life left. He was frail and weak; dying. Preparations had already begun for the coronation of his son."

Tom asked, "Well, what went wrong? Didn't Zeduza agree with her brother becoming King?"

"Worse than that. She decided to prevent him. Now, waiting around for him to die wasn't an option; the turning of the years was but a heartbeat for the Sweltian. No, Zeduza did something far more drastic. In the dead of night, she sneaked up on her brother whilst he slept, and…"

A pause; a pause which seemed to last an age. "Well? What did she do?" Doc chipped in again.

"She cut off his head. She then had her bodyguards dispose of the body, by burying it, far out in the forests of Maktem-Groll. All, that is, except for the head."

"Oh, gross," Jazz moaned. "What did she do with the head?"

The expression on the Caveman's face was grave. "She took it to a shaman, a magician of the dark arts who, to cut a tragic story short, *shrank* the head and stripped away the skin. As a final insult to the young man – her own brother – she had a golden chain attached to the miniature skull…" The archaic Caveman stopped speaking, as he realized that the significance of his words had slowly sunk in to the brains of the assembled children. "Yes," he proceeded once more, "The pendant that you unearthed…" He knew he didn't need to say more. "The King launched a great investigation, with a huge reward for any information on the whereabouts of his son, the crown prince. As a result, one of Zeduza's greedy bodyguards told the King what she had done."

"Did he get the reward?" Doc asked, always eager to hear of a scam.

"The only reward that he got was a fate worse than death, for his own part in the crime. Along with the other bodyguard, the king sentenced him to an eternity of crawling on the ground, as a reviled creature. He had both men turned into scurrying black scorpions."

Grim realization hit the children like a thunderbolt: she still had her horrible bodyguards protecting her, even to this day.

A dog could be heard howling, off in the distance, through the open window. It sounded like it was crying in despair. Doc felt the hairs on the back of his neck stand up, and he went over and closed the window against the chill night.

"She was expelled from the kingdom, sealed forever, in a huge sphere of rock. This rock was sent hurtling out of the Sweltian solar system," the Caveman stopped speaking; the children could see he was turning over something unpleasant in his mind.

"So...How did she end up on Earth, chasing after us, for her horrid necklace?" Tom asked.

"Well, it was probable that, sooner or later, the rock would collide with something. The odds were that it would smash into some remote planet in the middle of nowhere, or it would hook into some gravitational orbit and just continue round and round for evermore..."

"But?" Jazz asked the question, though deep down she didn't really want to hear the answer.

"But," the ancient one spoke slowly, "she defied the odds. She smashed into planet Earth, over a million years ago."

"Oh, Jazz," whispered Tom, "We have to get rid of that thing. Perhaps if we return it to her, she'll go back where she came from and leave us alone." He sounded about as convinced as the rest of them looked.

Doc was shaking his head, like he had a fly buzzing round him, and he looked more puzzled than ever. "But, hang on. This just doesn't add up. If all this happened so long ago, how come she's just got round to waking up? And," (the big question that had been forming in all their minds since this old giant's first appearance) "Where do you fit in all this? Who are you – and how come you know about all this stuff. Unless…"

Tom stood up and started backing away to the far side of the room. "Unless you're in on it with her," he said, voice quavering.

A quick tap – and the bedroom door opened. Doc's dad peered in. "Everything okay? All right for drinks?"

The full glasses of juice and untouched biscuits answered his question, but Doc knew that wasn't the real reason he had come up. Dad's parental radar was going full throttle. Doc's stunned expression took Dad by surprise, but the boy managed a "Fine, Dad, thanks."

"Well, if you need anything." Dad left the room, closing the door behind him.

If Dad had looked, he would have seen that both Tom and Jazz wore equally shocked expressions. As soon as the door had opened, the

Caveman had disappeared, as mysteriously and swiftly as he had arrived. The room felt like a vacuum. If the children hadn't witnessed it with their own eyes, they would have been convinced they'd dreamed it.

And now, there was a void where the primitive giant had been; a void, the children feared, that might lead to final and fatal danger, if they made the mistake of straying too close.

Chapter 20

The horrendous necklace nestled in the top drawer in Doc's dad's study. It had been a hard decision to arrive at, but the children had agreed they should hand it back over; if there was any chance that the university could learn more about the strange materials it was made from, then perhaps there might be a way to work out how to defeat the monster-woman, known as Zeduza.

There hadn't been the usual cheery 'goodbye-see-you-tomorrows' that were normally exchanged, when Tom and Jazz had left Doc's house that night. The children looked tired and drawn; the stress of the day had taken its toll on them all. When Mrs Studd had tucked Doc up for the night, kissing him lightly on the cheek, he had turned quietly over, and muffled into his pillow, "'Night, Mum," instead of nagging for just five more minutes with the light on.

Both Doc's mum and dad talked hard until almost midnight. The events of recent days had obviously had a very bad effect on Doc – and they knew that it was all connected to the mysterious pendant. They decided it would be time to get the *whole* story from their son, the very next morning, after they had all had a good night's sleep.

But the night didn't turn out at all the way they had planned.

* * *

Doc's dreams were plagued by terrible visions. He had finally fallen asleep, sometime after midnight, with a thousand questions flying around in his head, like vampire bats on the hunt.

Who was this ancient stranger, really? Did he mean to help them or to harm them? And how was it that he could speak so well, when cave men were supposed to only be able to grunt? Where was the screeching, swooping monster-woman hiding out just now? Could she simply be waiting for him to fall asleep, before smashing in with her grotesque bodyguards, stealing the necklace, and killing them all in their beds..?

No surprise then, that he was having vivid nightmares. In his dreams he stood on a bleak alien planet, in near-darkness, surrounded by withered trees adorned with skulls, like scary Christmas trees. In the near distance, just out of his range of vision in the murky gloom, he could hear awful clattering and clacking sounds, as if some insane old lady were knitting at a furious rate. He knew, however, that these sounds heralded the scorpion guards, and came from where they lurked…

The she-creature leapt from the darkness – a demon jack-in-the-box, with blazing hair and laser eyes. She screeched that soul-shuddering screech!

Then the scene changed.

He was now in a forest that was thick with vegetation. The richness of sounds was almost overwhelming, but not frightening. He saw massive shapes skulking in the distance. A silvery stream trickled close-by. His eyes were drawn to the stream. By the water's-edge sat a large, muscular man, similar to the Caveman who had visited them earlier in the night…but much, much younger. He had a mane of flowing black hair and a lush beard. In his hand he held a wicked-looking spear, with its point directed at the surface of the stream. He was hunting for fish. But something broke his concentration. The scene changed again. Time had shifted on. Now the man stood, trapped, with a wicked-looking dinosaur on either side of him. But he looked to the sky – and within an instant had been obliterated by a howling meteorite.

In his dream, Doc stared at the smoking hole where the man had been. And the scene altered once more. The jungle morphed into the present day scene of Raingate Cemetery. And right where the Caveman had just been so unexpectedly wiped out, a rickety old tomb reclined.

This is where Jazz found the necklace! The exact place where the meteorite crashed to Earth! In his slumbering mind, Doc had experienced this revelation.

A hand on his shoulder now. "You have to trust me. Your life and the lives of your friends depend upon it." Was he still dreaming? He felt kind of half and half. If he *was* dreaming, he was dreaming that he was lying in bed, in his own room. A dark figure, clad in animal skins leaned over him, with a rough old hand on his shoulder. Doc wondered whether he should scream. He couldn't, so the decision didn't have to be made.

The gravelly voice came again: "You saw how I perished, beneath the burning rock. You have seen it – and I have spoken it. You need not fear me."

Doc's words came slowly, like treacle dripping from a spoon. Like dream-speak. "How? How can you speak when you're dead? A dead cave man?"

A plop of water from across the room. *Davros?* "Am I really awake? Or am I dreaming you? Or…" A petrifying thought took centre-stage in Doc's head, "Or am I already dead?"

The bearded colossus laughed dryly. "No, little one. You are alive. I speak to you from beyond the barrier of death. There are far more dead people in the world than living. It was not very hard to find one who can speak, to channel my thoughts into words, so that I can communicate with you. I simply use his speech, as I would scratch pictures on the cave wall, to communicate my thoughts and feelings."

"You're using another dead guy's voice?"

"Of course; prehistoric men did not possess the power of speech."

Smoke. The unmistakable odour of smoke. A faint orange glow suggested itself in the tiny gaps around Doc's bedroom door.

Doc sat bolt upright in his bed. His heart thumped wildly; some deep-rooted instinct told him this was no dream!

The gnarled Caveman backed slowly away. "She is near… The key to her destruction…" He pointed a dusty finger towards the tank in which Davros resided. And with that the hairy giant faded into the night.

"What do you..?" Doc didn't get chance to finish his question, for two reasons: one, the Caveman had disappeared again and, two, his bedroom door had burst into flames.

Chapter 21

Doc leapt from his bed and threw open his bedroom window. Big mistake! This simply added oxygen-fuel to the already hungry flames. He ran this way and that, in a state of confusion, his head still fuggy with sleep.

He had two choices: he could risk making an exit through the open window - although the front lawn seemed an *awfully* long way down - or he could attempt to get through the burning doorway. Somehow, he didn't really fancy either option. The wind had gathered momentum outside and the flames fanned up quickly. Whatever it was that Doc was going to do, he had to do it quickly – or this really was the end.

An almighty crash! The door to Doc's bedroom tumbled inwards like a felled tree. He could see nothing out on the landing except swirling smoke and whips of orange flame. He was just able to make out the figures of Mum and Dad, on the far side of the landing; they were shouting and waving their arms. Dad dropped to a crouch and ran forward to Doc to try and save him, but was driven back by the ferocity of the flames; such was the speed that the conflagration had ripped into life. The blaze was so violent that there might just as well have been a raging dragon between parents and boy.

"Get to the window! I'll catch you!" Doc heard Dad's bellowed words, even above the roaring of flames and the cracking of timbers. It sounded like the whole house could fall down at any moment.

The intense heat made Doc's skin sting – and he didn't need persuading to obey Dad and head for the coolness of the window. As he gazed out and down, however, he felt his stomach lurch, as vertigo gripped him like a bully. He scooped up his glasses from the bedside table and, placing them on his nose, he looked down again. If anything, it appeared worse, now he could focus!

In another dimension – or so it felt – he heard Mum screaming for him to jump; Dad must have already charged downstairs to get beneath the window. This was confirmed as Doc saw him appear, seemingly a million miles below. Dad's voice had more clarity now, and no less urgency: "Jump, Daniel!"

Doc put both hands on the ledge, his limbs feeling rubbery, and placed one bare foot on the window sill. His dad nodded frantically, silently telling him that he was doing the right thing. Dad's desperate, yet hopeful expression evaporated, as Doc suddenly turned away and disappeared from the window.

"Daniel! Get out of there!" he yelled with all his heart.

In the bedroom, one of the walls had collapsed entirely in the rampant fire and the place felt like a furnace! But Doc had a task that he instinctively felt he had to do. He dived to the floor. It was easier to breathe down there, as the smoke swirled mainly overhead. The sound of a hundred roaring tigers filled his ears as he scrabbled around with his hand, underneath the bed. His fingers closed around what he sought, and he withdrew it swiftly. The plastic container was about fifteen centimetres tall by ten centimetres wide. Doc unscrewed the lid, with rising panic in his stomach, as he smelt the horrible odour of burning paint and wood. He emptied out his Dr Who cards and – so desperate was his plight – left them scattered on the floor. He skittered over to the fish tank and plunged the container into the water. He missed his target entirely but struck lucky on his second attempt. Peering into the murk, he could see Davros sploshing around in the jar, looking none-too-pleased. Doc hastily screwed the lid back on and made it back to the window in record time.

As he hoisted himself up onto the precipitous ledge, he gripped the jar tightly. Davros might be peeved, but at least he wasn't going to be fried fish tonight. As he prepared himself to jump, he took a deep, shuddering breath; he knew full well that he might not survive the leap intact. He howled at the top of his voice, ready to thrust himself forward. As he did so, a flare of yellow flame erupted from the collapsed wall to his left – the wall that had separated his bedroom from Dad's study. In a reflex action, he glanced quickly sideways, as he began to pitch forward from the window and into the cold night.

As he plummeted down, he forgot all about the danger of the leap for life. All that was stuck in the core of his brain was the image of the blazing study.

And the sight of the figure standing serenely in the heart of the raging blaze.

Chapter 22

A blissfully cold breeze whispered around Doc's face. He was half-sitting up, being cradled around the shoulders. His bottom was damp, and he blurrily realized that he was sitting on a wet grass verge. He had lost consciousness for a couple of minutes, as a result of the shock of the jump and the jarring bump of landing in Dad's arms.

The night was in chaos: the air was a tapestry of mixed smells; the unmistakable soapy scent of Mum, the raw odour of exhaust fumes, and the acrid stench of burning and smoke. Sounds cluttered his ears, each one competing for attention in his brain; creaks and crashes came from the blazing house, the cold wind sang eerily, his Mum babbled reassurances to him, and rain pattered heavily on the pavement. But there was a stronger sound of water – a gushing sound now that joined the others and came from the same place as a great roaring engine. Doc craned his head around and saw the huge red beast of the fire engine, with its swirling blue lights.

Firemen directed a fat snake of a hose at the inferno-house. In the noisy madness, recent events began to resurface in Doc's memory. In so doing, the grim realization hit him, that he could easily have been dead by now. He wrapped his arms round Mum and buried his head into her shoulder, as tears flowed. Mum shushed and patted his back, but didn't speak; mums have a way of setting things right without saying a word sometimes. She just hugged him right back, and let his heaving sobs slowly subside; an island in this ocean of craziness.

* * *

It was a long time before Doc withdrew from the safety of Mum's arms. When he did so, a familiar figure was standing a few metres away, surveying the damp, smoking remains of what had been the Studds' home. The fireman, who had given them all blankets to wrap themselves warmly in, had a sad expression; the entire upper storey of the house was a blackened wreck. The predominant sounds of the night were now the rapid 'drip-drip-drip' of dirty water coming down from the house, the murmuring of wakened neighbours, who seemed to be almost as stunned as Doc and his parents, and the icy dead-hours wind, moaning through the trees and the charcoal timbers of the house.

The fireman was Tom's dad. He held his helmet in his hands now, as he walked across to Doc and Mum, and Dad, who was looking ashen.

"I'll run you through to Casualty, in the engine. You really ought to get checked out, and I don't think either of you ought to be driving, in case of shock," Mr Allerton said, his voice heavy with concern.

"Thanks," replied Dad, "I think Daniel may need an x-ray; that was a big jump down from his bedroom."

"I'm fine," Doc interjected, but he winced and grunted a little as he spoke, and that was more than enough confirmation for Mum that an x-ray was *indeed* a good idea.

"Thank you, Ted," she said, standing up and helping Doc to his feet too. Something about the way she uttered the words made Doc realize that it would be futile to argue.

On any other occasion, Doc would have been thrilled to be given a ride in the fire engine, but tonight he felt tired, numb. The crew shuffled up and, though it was a bit of a squeeze, Doc found himself snug between Mum and Dad, as the engine roared forward.

His thoughts inescapably returned to the moments before he made his death-defying leap. He vividly recalled the tumbling bedroom wall that opened a fiery gateway to Dad's study. He recalled the twisting tongues of orangey-yellow flame and the billowing black smoke. He recalled perching on the ledge, like a strange fledgling bird ready to take flight. And he recalled – most clearly of all – the serene figure looking out at him from the conflagration, arm outstretched. He had thought it was beckoning to him, until the object which it had thrown landed skilfully in his pyjama jacket pocket.

The Caveman had made the impossible shot. The skull-necklace nestled, even now, on the journey to hospital, in Doc's top pocket. He never even considered telling Mum and Dad about this occurrence; he knew that the Caveman had placed it back in his keeping for a reason. The horrible, hellish thing had to be returned to its horrible, hellish owner. Only then, Doc believed, would there be a possibility that this waking nightmare would end.

He peered into the night. New rain slithered down the

windscreen, creating a kaleidoscope effect with the streetlamps and the murky darkness. As they rounded a bend in the road, Doc saw a shimmering figure, standing… watching… Flames snaked madly about its head and its face was twisted into a snarl. Doc took an involuntary, sharp inhalation.

"Doc? What is it?" Mum sounded alarmed.

He blinked. And the figure was gone. Just an eerie dark space remained, where the monster had been.

"Nothing," Doc responded, but he dug himself deeper into Mum's protective body and held tight to the plastic jar in which Davros swam nervously. "Nothing… It's okay."

But he knew that the creature had tried to kill them all in their beds tonight.

And the weird necklace suddenly felt uncomfortably warm in his pyjama pocket, beneath the camouflaging cover of the blanket, wrapped tightly around his upper body.

Chapter 23

After getting checked over at the hospital – Doc had nothing more serious than mild bruising (at least, physically) – Mum, Dad and a very exhausted Doc, arrived at Grandma Studd's house, where they had hot cocoa before hitting welcome soft beds.

Mum and Dad were all for letting Doc take the day off school; it had been 3 a.m. before they were able to get to sleep. But Doc had insisted – even after great attempts at persuasion from his parents – that he wanted to go.

"To take my mind off things," he had said and, at this, Mum and Dad had reluctantly agreed.

Mum had gathered together a few essentials from the pretty-well untouched downstairs of their burnt house prior to going to the hospital, so Doc had his school clothes on well in advance of setting-off time. His seemingly-cheery wave goodbye from Grandma's gate didn't fool anyone. All three adults would be counting the minutes till he returned home that night, and Mum had decided she would phone school at lunchtime to check on him. Dad agreed, and he'd contacted the Uni to explain that he wouldn't be in today.

When he was out of sight of Grandma's, Doc dropped the fake smile and hurried on to meet up with Tom and Jazz as usual, for their walk to school. The morning was dank and cheerless, reflecting his own mood, but at least the chill wind blew away some of the dusty cobwebs that hung around in his sleep-starved head.

* * *

The walk to school with his best friends had been mercifully uneventful; no ambushes from she-monsters and giant scorpion guards today. The buzz of conversation, however, had been intense.

"It's lucky you woke up, mate," Tom had concern in his voice. "You could easily've been killed." He looked earnestly at Doc. No wisecracks or bravado came back in response.

"Too right I could. *And* my entire family," Doc asserted, his face set in a frown. But there was something else in his face today. Jazz could see. His features were etched with a grim determination. That's why his next words came as no surprise.

"This *thing*," he drew the necklace roughly out of his pocket, "is going right back where it came from. Back where it belongs in that graveyard." He stopped dead in his tracks and regarded his friends with a stony expression. "I know I had stupid ideas about making money from it and all that, but I just didn't see the danger…"

"It's okay," Jazz said, "None of us could have realized what would kick off from this."

"Well," Doc stated firmly, "I'm getting rid of it tonight, and you can either help me or not. Believe me, I'll understand if you want to stay out of it."

"Hey. We're in this as a team," Tom interjected. "Whatever we do, we do together. But…"

"No buts – it's going back tonight." Doc snapped.

"No, mate. That's not what I was going to say. Yes, it does have to go back. And tonight's as good a time as any. But I think it's gonna take more than planting the necklace back in that grave hole to solve the problem that's on our backs."

Jazz and Doc stared at Tom, with curiosity. But they were all ears.

"We have to find a way of getting round that fiery witch, too. Or she'll do for all of us."

Jazz spoke decisively: "That's it then. Meet up at my place after tea. By then, we'll have come up with some ideas. Or not… Either way, we need to prepare – and we can see the graveyard from my attic window. Agreed?"

The boys nodded. "But, how are you going to get your mum and dad to let you out tonight? They won't allow it, Doc," warned Tom.

"Leave that to me. I'll be there, all right? Even if it means breaking every rule in the book. Our lives are at stake."

The crow that decided to screech and flap off from the spindly branches overhead, right at that very moment, did nothing to soothe their collective sense of fear.

Chapter 24

As Doc stepped into Gran's hallway, just after 4 o'clock, Mum bundled him into her arms and squeezed him tight.

"How did your day go?" she asked, then before giving him time to answer, she added, "I called school to make sure you were okay, at lunchtime. Hope you don't mind, sweetheart."

Doc did his best to sound reassuring, and he didn't fib, as he replied, "Fine. It was fine, Mum. I'm just really tired." The, oh-so gorgeously *safe* smell of his favourite spag bol emanated from Gran's kitchen, accompanied by her smiling face. "Hi Gran. Hi Dad," he broke free of Mum and went over to give big hugs to the other two adults.

"Tea's nearly ready. Why don't you nip up and get changed, son?" Dad patted his shoulder and, as the boy padded off upstairs, exchanged relieved glances with both Mum and Gran.

Daniel was home and safe. And – although they knew full well he could suffer delayed shock at some point – at least he was where they could keep an eye on him again. For now, that was all that mattered to them.

* * *

Mum took one last look at Doc, then Dad ushered her from the bedroom, whispering, "Let him rest, love. He's absolutely shattered. Chances are he'll sleep the clock round, and we won't hear anything more from him till morning."

Mum smiled and blew a silent kiss to her son, who lay snuggled and warm beneath a huge duvet, in the gathering darkness of the bedroom. As the door clicked shut, Doc's eyes flicked open. The luminous red digits of the bedside clock read: 5:46. Exhausted as he was, sleep was the very last thing on Doc's mind. Adrenaline raced through his veins and outlandish plans fluttered round his brain, like moths to a flame.

He had taken the heart-wrenching decision to go behind his parents' backs; the situation was - to him - so serious.

Doc's first challenge would be to get out of the house without being discovered. In all the recent excitement, he really hadn't considered how to achieve this. If he tried to sneak downstairs, he'd be toast before he even reached the bottom; in Gran's house the stairs led straight into the open plan living room. So that option was out, unless he waited until about midnight, when they were all asleep – and by that time, it would be too late. The only other available choice was to leave via the bedroom window… Doc grimaced at the thought, as the memory of last night's leap of faith slammed into his brain. He remembered seeing an old film once, where a prisoner escaped from jail by tying bed sheets together and abseiling down the wall to the ground. But if he did that, as soon as anyone looked in on him, they'd notice straight away.

The situation appeared hopeless. As Tom had said earlier, there was absolutely no way that his mum and dad would give him permission to go out tonight. He lay there in the now complete darkness; his bedside clock had raced round to 5:59 – and his heart raced with it. He had half an hour at the most to get to Tom and Jazz, or they'd assume (probably rightly) that he was unable to get out.

He made his mind up then; the old bed sheet routine, it had to be. He scrambled out of bed as quickly and quietly as he could and pulled off the bottom sheet. He twined it round till it resembled a Tarzan vine, only way too short, then he stripped the cover off the duvet and did the same with that. Muffled T.V sounds filtered up the stairs, along with the serious-sounding voices of his family. Sweat dampened his forehead, even though the cool air of early evening reached in through the open window like deathly fingers.

It was whilst he was attempting to tie the ends of the sheet and the duvet cover together, that Doc became aware of the change in the sounds from downstairs. Louder. The T.V still mumbled on, but his mum's voice had become increased in volume. This meant one of two things: either she had got really angry and was starting to raise her voice - which she hardly ever did - or she was getting closer!

The creaking of the stairs gave the unwelcome answer – Mum was coming up the stairs. Her built-in parental radar had decided it was time for a check. Thoughts rushed round his head in panic. *Should he try to cover himself quickly in the twisted bedclothes, and hope she wouldn't notice in the dark? Risky! Should he try to untangle them and make the bed? Impossible!! Should he…*

This last thought never reached a conclusion. The bedroom door swung inwards. Soft light from the landing bathed him in its glow, and he froze, crouched over the bed linen in mid-knot.

"Daniel! What on Earth do you think you're-"

Doc fully expected a force-10 blasting from Mum at this point. But it never came. The oncoming storm of her anger simply fizzled and stopped. Absolute silence in mid-sentence.

Then Mum sort of wobbled, like a feather in a breeze, and fell to the floor, in an apparent faint.

"Mum!" Doc yelled, and rushed across to see if he could help her. Then "Dad! Gran!" he hollered through the open bedroom door.

As he bent over Mum, gently shaking her by the shoulder and saying her name over and over, he – dimly at first, then with a tumultuous realization – became aware that *all* sound in the house had ceased, save for his own fading voice, the hammering of his heart, and the murmuring television.

Simultaneously, something else rushed in on his consciousness.

He was not alone with Mum in the room.

In the periphery of his vision, by the softly billowing curtains, framed by the darkness of the open window, a figure stood. Watching. Doc closed his eyes, sensing all hope was lost. He just prayed it would be over quickly.

Chapter 25

Jazz chewed her thumb nail nervously and glanced up at the clock. "It's nearly half past. He's not gonna make it, is he?"

"It's looking that way. I guess his parents have got the eagle eye on him." Tom paced the room like a caged tiger. He cracked his knuckles, absent-mindedly, even though his mum had said he'd get arthritis if he carried on. "Still – we'll give him a few more minutes before we give up on the idea…" He stopped his pacing as he reached the attic room window.

The night outside looked inky and threatening. The once-enticing graveyard sprawled beyond the large wall, a monstrous garden of dead things, punctuated with the jagged teeth of gravestones and tombs. A chill ran through Tom's bones and he tried to push the image from his mind. He deliberately gazed further into the distance, only to be met with the unsettling sight of Sandal Castle, cold and dark against the horizon. Tonight, it was a giant, hunched-up ghoul – squat and black. It crouched in the gloom, waiting for victims to stray into its cold embrace.

Tom turned around to soak in the welcome light of the attic once more, but found that the grim thoughts in his head were unwilling to fade into the shadows. Jazz sighed heavily and inserted the nail of an index finger into the space just vacated by her thumb. A horrible silence draped itself over the room; it was the kind of silence that made you feel sick; the kind of silence you could cut with a knife; the kind of silence that feeds on hopelessness.

And it was the kind of silence that was made all the more frightening when it was broken by a sudden rapping at the front door downstairs.

Urgent. Hurried. Almost frantic.

Jazz's eyes bulged wide as she stared at Tom, questioningly.

Tom hesitated. A wicked voice in his head insisted that the monsters had finally come to get them. That Doc had already fallen victim. And that there was no escape for them now. Then he resolved that the only thing to do was to get downstairs, open that door – and face his deepest fear.

Chapter 26

Tom flung the door open wide and in rushed a great, icy blast of wind. He took an involuntary gasp at the chilliness of the air - and blinked rapidly. There on the doorstep, looking flustered but very much alive, stood Doc. Tom blinked again. Then let out a long sigh of relief.

"You letting me in, or what?"

Doc's impatient tone broke the spell that Tom temporarily found himself in. He stepped aside, hurriedly saying, "Come in!"

Jazz appeared at the top of the steep stairwell, grinning broadly and clapping her hands in delight at the sight of Doc. Then she realized just how seriously uncool she must have looked and stopped at once, adopting a casual lean against the banister and muttering, "What kept you?"

Once settled in the relative safety of the attic, Doc explained the reason for his delay and – indeed – the reason for his arrival.

* * *

"You mean, they're under some kind of spell?" Jazz looked baffled.

Doc spread his hands and shook his head. "Spell… hypnosis… an influence of some sort… I don't know. All I do know is that, one minute Mum steps through the door, and I know – just *know* – that I'm caught red-handed, with my hands full of twisted sheet and duvet; the

98

next moment, she's spark out on the floor, like an earthquake wouldn't wake her up." He stopped speaking, looking intently at both Tom and Jazz, before letting out a deep breath and continuing. "And there he was – *him* – standing by the window. Heaven only knows how he got there…"

"The Caveman," Tom nodded, prompting his friend to go on.

"Yep. And he says they're all asleep: Mum, Dad *and* Gran – and they won't know anything till gone midnight. But they're safe and sound and won't know a thing about it afterwards. He says that's all the time we've got though; his magic can't keep them all under any longer. So we'd better sort out what we're gonna do."

Jazz was clean out of Coke (her parents were away on a trip again) so she poured them all a glass of fizzy water and they sat pondering the next move.

Tom sipped thoughtfully. "Okay," he said, "Doc, you've brought the necklace?" Doc dug into his jeans pocket and dangled the pendant. The grisly little skull spun around ominously, as if trying to stare at them all at once, or hypnotise them.

"So we can take that back where it came from," Tom said, inclining his head towards the window and the gruesome graveyard beyond.

"Should take about five minutes," Jazz stated, trying to reassure herself.

"Sure. But we know that's not all. We have to find a way of getting round that monster, don't we?" Tom frowned.

"And fast," Doc supportively added.

"Aw, man, there's no way we can beat her. She's just too powerful; she'll be waiting for us. And as soon as she gets that horrible thing back," Jazz pointed at the necklace, tears threatening her eyes, "she might kill the lot of us." She stood up and strode away to the window, in an attempt to disguise her distress. As she did so, she accidentally kicked the open bottle of sparkling water and it spilled over, staining the light wood floor a darker shade.

Tom got to his feet and said, "I'll sort it out, don't worry. Where d'you keep the cloths?"

But before Jazz could even attempt to answer, Doc made them both jump out of their skins, by shouting: "No! Leave it!" He gazed at the pool of water, which spread like a darkening blood clot. Jazz turned sharply from the window at Doc's bizarre outburst, but something in his expression – in his eyes – stopped her from saying anything. Tom detected that same look; Doc's eyes were *fixated* on the spillage. Either he'd lost the plot for good now, or…

Doc leaned forward, clicking his fingers and pointing at the water. "Could it be possible?"

He stood up.

Paced around.

Put his hands on his head.

Spread his arms wide.

Moved his lips soundlessly, as if having a silent conversation with some invisible person.

The pendant still swung in his grasp.

"Doc?" Tom ventured, only to be met with the 'shushing' gesture of a raised palm from Doc. He then dangled the necklace over the mini-lake of water, and it began to spin furiously, the overhead lights sending reflective shimmers around the walls.

And he smiled. *That* smile. That - *Doc's-just-thought-of-something* – smile.

And Tom and Jazz didn't know whether to sigh with relief, or get up and run – as far away as they possibly could. They didn't run.

Chapter 27

Doc looked, wide-eyed, at his friends. His expression said: *Don't you see?* Tom screwed his face up in puzzlement, whilst Jazz spread her hands palms upwards and shook her head.

"Watch…" Doc lowered the shrunken skull over the wet patch and – impossible though it was – the little head seemed to be pulling away from the water, like two north poles on a magnet. But gravity had its way and, when the yellow-bone pendant contacted the water, a plume of hissing steam jetted angrily into the air.

Tom's face was now a mask of concentration, as his eyes flicked from the necklace to Doc. "Go on, Doc. Time's running out. If you've worked out a way of beating this thing, you'd best tell us now." Jazz flapped her hands in agreement, gesturing for Doc to hurry.

"Okay," Doc began, "Remember the first time you realized something weird was going on?"

Jazz nodded. "Yeah… at the swimming pool."

"You knew you were in danger, you saw the monster's shadow coming at you. And the skull heated up." He paused briefly. "What did you do to get rid of that threat?"

"Went for a swim?" Tom questioned, still looking puzzled.

"Exactly! And then when we got ambushed up here in the attic, with those horrible cockroach things, and the giant scorpions, and the monster woman…" Doc tilted his head on one side, waiting for the penny to drop for his friends. He certainly had their attention, and Jazz seemed deep in thought, her expression difficult to read.

"The sprinkler system," Jazz murmured – and she scrambled to her feet, rushing from the room, leaving the door swinging behind her and scurrying down the stairs.

"What's up with her?" Doc said.

"She's probably just freaked, thinking about that night," Tom suggested.

A sudden gust of wind rattled the window in its frame, as if something dreadful was trying to get inside. Tom shuddered, but Doc was on a roll. The lights dimmed, then brightened again, as Doc concluded, "Then in the woods, on the way to school. She had us all trapped, didn't she?"

"And it poured with rain!" Tom blurted.

"WATER!" the two boys yelled simultaneously.

At that precise moment, a shadow materialized in the doorway, making the boys' hearts miss a beat. As they turned, they were relieved to see that it was Jazz, returned from wherever she had been. She stood upright, legs akimbo, with a wicked grin on her face. In each hand she held a massive *'Super-Soaker-Master-Blaster'*, the hugest water-squirter rifles the boys had ever set eyes on.

Tom looked at Doc, then at Jazz, and back to Doc again. "Are you thinking what I'm thinking?" he said, the ghost of a smile playing on his lips. Doc's eyes were sparkling like fires.

Jazz raised the soakers high in the air. "Lock – and *load!*" she sang.

Outwardly, the boys displayed great delight that the old Jazz – the confident, the eccentric, the manic Jazz – was back. Inwardly, little voices nagged away at them both. Jazz was back; and if she ran true to form, it could lead to a whole mountain of trouble!

Chapter 28

The moon was a bright circular blade in a jet black sky. It peered down through scurrying clouds, at the night-clad Earth. Far below its cold eye, the terrain spread out in uneven patterns. The shimmering lake in Pugney's Water Park reflected thousands of miniature moons. The hunched back of Sandal Castle's ruin rose from the ground, as if ready to pounce. The ominous Crematorium chimney lanced upwards, dark and gloomy. And, sprawled in the midst of amber street-lights and clusters of houses – the domain of the living – protruded the jagged tombstone teeth of Raingate Cemetery, the domain of the dead.

Four indistinct figures lurked in the darkness: two were long and low, with distorted limbs – scorpionesque; two possessed vaguely human forms.

If the moon had been sentient, it might also have perceived three smaller figures – perhaps children – stealthily enter the outskirts of the graveyard. Two of them carried large objects in their arms.

If the moon had ears, it might have heard their hearts hammering.

If the moon had a voice, it would have shouted the warning, to turn and run for their lives.

Chapter 29

On this occasion, Doc had drawn the short straw. He picked his way through the gravestones, with the necklace clutched in his sweaty left palm. In his right he had a small yellow water pistol - *which might just put a candle out, on a good day* - thought Doc. Backing him up, with the massive Super-Soakers, were Tom and Jazz, some distance behind; one to the left, flitting through shadowy old tree trunks, one to the right, moving along the outer wall of the cemetery, like a ghost.

Tom felt hemmed-in by the cold heights of the trees, but reassured a bit by the heaviness of the water-filled blaster in his hands.

The wind whistled through the spindly branches, cracked gravestones, and fractured sepulchres. Doc, flanked by the loyal Tom and Jazz, tried not to think of it as being the icy breath of dead people. He was particularly jittery because he was the only one without a *Super-Soaker-Master-Blaster.* "I've only got two of them," Jazz had explained; so they tossed coins – odd one out got to put the necklace back whilst the other two acted as cover. The plan was then to soak the monster-woman with every drop from the guns – *if* she appeared – and then run like lightning, in the hope that once she'd got her nasty pendant back, she'd leave them all alone and go back where she came from.

Tom glanced across to see Jazz slithering along the wall; he knew she would be filled with guilt and blaming herself for all this. *Here was Doc, in very real danger, trying to put back what never should have been taken.*

But then, thought Tom, *none of us are blameless in all this.* Doc was the one who wanted to hang on to the necklace, just that bit longer… And Tom couldn't excuse himself from the blame: *If only I'd tried harder – insisted we put it back. Maybe this wouldn't be happening.*

His glance diverted to Doc, who was getting closer – ever closer – to the ruined tomb where the necklace had been found. Tom tightened his grip on the Super-Soaker. The night was still and cold. Not a cloud in the sky. This revealed the target tomb in its full, ruined glory. It was a kaleidoscope of debris, chunks of mossy stone all weirdly heaped up. But it still had gaps in the jigsaw of rubble - gaps that could easily conceal something sinister, something horrible… Doc was so close now that he would soon be able to reach out his hand and drop the rotten thing back into the ghastly dead mouth of the grave. As he watched Doc take his last few tentative steps to the sepulchre, Tom was relieved to observe that there was no sign of a flame-headed monster-woman lurking around in the graves. Then – over there to Tom's left, on the periphery of his vision, he detected movement in a thick clump of bushes, by the opposite wall to where Jazz was creeping along. In the pale moonlight, this cluster of shrubs formed the only gloomy patch in Tom's field of vision. Yet he could certainly make out something… Something was disturbing the foliage. The dry leaves rustled – and a twig cracked. And for a fraction of a second, Tom saw a head emerge from the vegetation; a split second that instantly burned itself into Tom's mind… The head was covered in a mass of writhing…

Releasing one hand from his super-soaker, Tom reached into his jeans pocket for his mobile phone. His heart walloped, and his hand was moist with sweat, as he speed-dialled Jazz's number.

* * *

Jazz took a sharp intake of breath as her mobile vibrated, like an angry, ethereal wasp. She tucked the water blaster under her arm and pulled the agitated mobile from her hip pocket; the photo of a grinning Tom was displayed as the caller-image, a reminder of easier times.

"Tom?" she whispered, struggling to keep the Super-Soaker under control and hold the phone at the same time, "What is it?"

"Get over to me, Jazz – quick. I've seen it. It's nowhere near the grave! It's hiding in some bushes by the far wall!" His voice sounded raspy and strained, as he attempted to half-whisper, half-shout.

Jazz peered across the crooked rows of tombs and could see him waving frantically at her. "Coming!" she briskly said, and clicked the mobile shut, half-pushing it back in her pocket. She grasped the water cannon in two hands and crossed the graveyard in a zigzaggy, crouching run. As she jinked between the crumbly crosses and dilapidated angels, her mobile jiggled out of her pocket and fell soundlessly into a nest of thistles. She was completely unaware; more important issues were on her mind. Within seconds, she was skidding to a halt by Tom's side.

Tom gestured with his soaker to the thicket and, sure enough, there was the tell-tale movement of the foliage again, and the brief outline of a head that seemed snake-covered. Both their hearts skipped a beat as they heard a horrible, angry growling sound emerge from the beast within the bushes. Then Jazz pulled herself up to her tallest height, looked Tom straight in the eye, and said, "Okay, Tom. If we're gonna put a stop to this – let's get it over and done with."

Tom nodded grimly. "Lock and load time, eh?"

"Lock and load," she replied, without the faintest hint of a smile or her characteristic bravado.

They both raised their Super-Soakers to chest height, pointing the barrels at the animated branches. Then – as if rehearsed and synchronized – they both yelled long and loud, and ran hell-for-leather at the thing in the bushes.

Chapter 30

Doc was two steps away from the awful, ruinous grave that had hidden the necklace for so many years. The moonlight-shadows formed by the stretching branches of the gnarled old trees, were sinister demons in the still cold night. The grave itself hid many dark recesses too. And it was in the heart of the darkest, deepest shadow of the broken tomb that Doc knew he must replace the pendant. He strained his eyes hard, trying to make out any detail, or potential threat inside the chasm of black, but his eyes couldn't help him; the blackness was so dense that he sensed he could almost touch it.

One step closer. He started to reach out, extending his arm as far as he dared, fearing that if he reached too far, the waiting darkness might devour his hand. He stared harder into the guts of the grave and fancied that he saw a swirling purple light, hypnotic and enticing. He took the last, involuntary step forward to the tomb, and felt himself being pulled towards the gaping shadow at its centre. The spiralling purplish light drew him, like metal to a magnet. The necklace itself, with its grinning little yellow head, tried to tug free from his hand like an unruly dog on a leash – straining, straining, always pulling to the heart of the tomb. The purple glow intensified in the surrounding darkness, like something from outer space, and Doc became dimly aware that clouds had ambushed the moon and kidnapped its light. It was as if one colossal shadow had swallowed him whole.

That's when he heard the yells. Tom and Jazz…

* * *

Water jetted out of the huge plastic guns like blood from torn arteries. Tom and Jazz had started blasting as soon as they were in range, screaming, firing and running all at the same time. The creature in the bushes howled like a mad dog and caused the branches to go this way and that, as it tried to dodge the powerful bursts of icy water.

The two friends skidded to a halt in a flurry of flying gravel, still shooting chilling streams of liquid from the Super-Soakers. "We've got her, Doc!" Tom bellowed, over Jazz's continued war cries. "Get rid of the necklace and get out of there!" Tom had no idea whether or not Doc had heard him in the chaos – but this was better than they could have hoped for! Soak her enough and they might even get rid of her for good. At least they'd make it out of the graveyard in one piece, as she steamed and cooled in the cannon fire of water.

They pumped and pumped, and fired and yelled. They weren't sure whether they were yelling to scare the monster-woman, or to cover up their own terror. Eventually, the thing in the bushes stopped jumping around, and went silent. Yet they carried on soaking the target area for a long time after, until even the mighty Super-Soakers were empty. For a while they shouted their anger and fear, and their fingers pressed triggers that clicked on empty barrels, until they were too exhausted to continue.

Jazz's arms dropped to her sides, and the plastic rifle hit the gravel path with a crunch. She looked at Tom. He was staring at the unmoving branches of the bushes, still clutching the empty soaker in his hands. He was shaking - not just with the chill of the night. His eyes turned upwards and gazed at the sky. Jazz followed his eye line and saw that he was looking at the bulbous black clouds that had smothered the moon, like a pack of wolves. Jazz had a sudden and inescapable feeling that something was terribly, terribly wrong. As she glanced again at Tom, she could see by his face that he felt it too. It was as if the darkness had closed around the cemetery like a gloved hand, and the silence pressed in like a vice.

The thing in the bushes growled ominously and started to emerge from the foliage, like a ghoul from a grave. As it began to reveal itself, the two friends felt an almost irresistible compulsion to run for their lives. But they stood fast, shoulder to shoulder, determined to see this through. If their logic had been correct, then they should have bought Doc enough time to return the pendant to its resting place, and this thing that was crawling from the sodden bush would be harmless in its drenched state. Furthermore, they hoped that it would drag itself to the tomb and slither in after its weird necklace, never to trouble them again – satisfied with the return of its prize.

Any glimmer of hope that the plan had worked at all was crushed as the thing from the bushes, with one last great push and a snarl, lunged itself out of the cover of branches and leaves and flopped down onto the gravelly ground right in front of their feet.

It stared up at them with red, angry eyes.

Chapter 31

Confusion and terror rushed in on them like a tidal wave.

The thing that had come out of the bush, although bedraggled from the attack of the Super-Soakers, had the same snake-like hair as the fire monster, but there were contradictions. The multi-coloured mane was plastered close to its head, but the eyes that stared up were not demonic; angry yes, demonic, no! These eyes were unmistakably human. The body itself was clad in a scruffy old black coat, from which protruded a soggy brown paper bag. From the top of this bag poked the neck of a glass bottle and, as the figure staggered to its feet, Tom and Jazz could hear some kind of liquid sloshing around inside.

Tom backed slowly away, as if being pushed by unseen hands, his eyes never leaving the strange, inexplicable figure which swayed unsteadily on its feet, water slopping from every part of it. But Jazz gave no ground. She stood as still as a rock, staring hard at the revelation before her.

"Jazz!" hissed Tom. ***"Come on!"***

But Jazz was unmoving. She had an expression on her face that was difficult for Tom to read; a look that gave the impression she was remembering something, very, very slowly but surely. Then her jaw went slack and her eyes gaped wide in grim realization.

"What?!" she whispered.

"What?" Tom appeared to mimic.

"Old Joe!" Jazz almost yelped.

"Hey! Yer've soaked me tae the skin, yer pair o' horrors!" growled the waterlogged figure, reaching into the soggy paper bag and tugging the whiskey bottle free.

The reality of the situation rushed in on Tom all at once, now. 'Old Joe' was the vagrant, the old tramp that roamed the local streets and fields always trying to persuade people to part with their 'loose change'. As the old man swigged from the amber whiskey in his bottle, the rage still burned in his red-streaked eyes and he grunted like a wounded animal.

Urgent, frightful questions surfaced in Tom's and Jazz's minds: *Why was Old Joe hiding in a bush in the graveyard? And why was his usually bald head covered in a mass of tangled, brightly-coloured, snaky hair?*

And worst of all, in the sudden gloom and cloying atmosphere of this midnight graveyard: *Whilst they had been engaged in soaking this shivering old man to the skin, what had happened to Doc, as he tried to return the frightful necklace to the broken tomb?*

An awful wall of silence and darkness was the only answer they got, as they looked across to the part of the graveyard where Doc should have been.

Chapter 32

Upon reaching the ruined tomb, the intended drop-off point for the hideous necklace, Tom and Jazz found empty space that seemed as vast as a universe. The rubble was still there, piled up like crumbling dominoes, and a strange sort of fog hung in the air; yet there was no sign of Doc – not even a clue. He had simply disappeared. They had called his name over and over, desperate to locate him, but they knew deep down that they were just shouting at the darkness; a darkness that seemed to be almost solid.

Old Joe had harangued them briefly, as they stumbled around in confusion, spluttering their own apologies to the old man. But how could they explain why they had soaked him through to the skin? They didn't even try. But as the old man got nearer to the smashed grave, his anger dissipated: he seemed filled with trepidation.

"She's evil, that one…" were the last words he muttered as he shuffled quickly away towards the cemetery exit. The children heard him take a deep swig from his whiskey bottle as he became cloaked by the shadows.

Jazz spread her arms wide in a gesture of self-defence, but Tom gravely murmured, "I don't think he means you, Jazz."

They stood, helpless and hopeless, in the heart of the gothic graveyard. Neither knew what to say or do. The urge to be sick rose strongly in both Tom and Jazz, as the wind began to stir, disturbing the fog around them; as it did, a familiar stench invaded their nostrils. It was the horrible smell that resembled rotting meat. Then they knew. They knew that the monster had somehow outwitted them. They sensed that the necklace was back in her clutches and – far worse – that their best friend may have been abducted. For all they knew, Doc might already be…

The unwelcome thought that battered at both their minds was cut harshly short by the strident ringing of Tom's mobile phone. As the Samsung vibrated and twittered in the pocket of his blue jeans, Tom's heart nearly leapt out of his chest, and Jazz gave an involuntary yelp of fright. Tom scrambled the mobile out of his pocket as rapidly as he could, fearing that the longer it rang, the more likely it was that something evil would come rushing at him in the dark.

His eyes were wide with shock, as he stared at the illuminated display screen. There, in shining letters, flashed the words: *Text message: Doc mobile.*

Chapter 33

Tom stared open-mouthed at the phone in his palm, as if it were some strange little alien. His mind was numb, unable to think clearly at all. *If Doc had been kidnapped by that terrible creature... How could he be texting?*

Jazz seemed to have read his mind, when she murmured: "Tom, what if it isn't Doc?" She saw the puzzlement on Tom's face, and added, "I know it's his *mobile* that's texting you... But what if something has taken it from him?"

The phone fell silent now, the text alert over. Somehow that was even worse than the insistent tweeting noise it had been making. Now the silence pressed in on them with the thick darkness and the cloying dead smell. They felt like they were suffocating.

"Tom. You'd better read the text."

Tom nodded slowly in agreement, then raised his glance to Jazz. "Okay," he said, "but let's get back out on the street first. I can't stand it in here a minute longer."

Just then, the moon forced a slice of silver between the clouds, like a torch beam, and in the periphery of his vision Tom saw something glint. It glistened yellowish in the darkness; just a hint of a sight, no more distinct than the touch of a cobweb. Tom squinted his eyes and Jazz turned to see what he was trying to focus on. Then the clouds masked the moon again – and the ghostly shimmer winked out.

Digging in her pocket for her mini-torch, Jazz flicked on the little light, and swung the beam slowly around in the general area where the glinting had been. The pair didn't speak – no words were needed. Deep down they both feared the truth of what they had seen. For several long moments, the torch alighted on nothing other than weeds, stones and gravel. Then –

There in the midst of long grass and nettles, was the glimmering yellow light. Tom strode forward, steeling his nerves as best he could. Disregarding the unpleasant stings from the wicked nettles that raked his flesh, he thrust his hand into the vegetation. His fingers touched something cold and, grasping it in his fist, Tom withdrew his hand quickly. He held the thing at arm's length as Jazz shone the torch light on it. They let out simultaneous sighs of relief, as they realised that the thing in Tom's hand was only a piece of reflective material, yellow and shiny – but certainly not metallic.

"It must have come off one of the workmen's coats, or something," Jazz suggested.

Tom made no reply; he just threw the harmless bit of material to the ground and snapped, "Let's get out of here."

Jazz took no persuading. Within a minute they had scurried from the graveyard and were out in the welcome halogen glare of street lights.

Chapter 34

Gasping, hearts thumping, Tom and Jazz stood beneath the halo of a street light in the relative safety of the road beside the cemetery. Everything seemed oddly quiet. Like the calm before a storm. Apart from the half-hearted barking of a dog, somewhere off in the distance over Pugney's way, and the whine of the now nagging wind, the only sounds they could hear were their own heartbeats, drumming away. Doubled over, they tried to regain their breath. It wasn't just the run from the graveyard that had taken their breath away; it was undiluted fear – fear of the monster, and what the future might soon bring.

Tom forced himself to straighten up, being only too aware of the mobile which sat, poisonous as a scorpion, in his hand. Without further delay, Tom pressed the 'options' button, then selected to view the text message. Jazz huddled in close and, as the strengthening breeze tugged at their coats, they read it. The message was brief, but its impact was powerful, like a blow to their stomachs:

Tom jazz. They got me. Go str8 to crem. Meet there 10 mins. No police or

There the text message ominously ended. Tom tried to scroll down, but there were no more words on the screen. Tom's mind was in danger of going into meltdown. He couldn't think. Couldn't focus. If they didn't go to the police, they were completely at the mercy of the creature and her terrible guards. If they did go to the police…

Tom knew, in his heart, what the unfinished text meant. The mobile slid from his hand and clattered to the pavement with a harsh sound that broke the spell of uncertainty - in Jazz, at least. She scooped up the phone, glancing at the screen, then checked her wristwatch. "That text came two minutes ago." She then jabbed an index finger in the general direction of the Crematorium, which was set back from the steeply-inclining road that led to Sandal Castle. "Which means," Jazz continued urgently, "we have about eight minutes to get there, or Doc…"

Jazz's incomplete sentence turned Tom's blood cold. "Run!" he yelled, and the two of them set off as if the hounds of Hell were on their tails, rather than something worse waiting for them at their destination. As they hurtled down the street, with the icy November wind stinging their eyes, Jazz stuffed Tom's mobile into her own pocket. Tom would have to wait till later to get it returned; there were more pressing issues right now.

* * *

Mr and Mrs Studd, and Grandma Studd, were entirely at peace. In the silence of Gran's house they slept on, blissfully unaware of the danger that Daniel was in. But – worse still – if they had been able to prevent him from leaving the house that evening, they may well have been asleep, permanently, with the house in ashes around them.

In a corner of the front room, as the TV continued to play quietly to its slumbering audience, stood an ancient weather-beaten figure, shaggy hair covering most of its face; but not the eyes. The eyes of the Caveman burned brightly-red, focusing hard to keep the spell intact on the sleepers. So focused was he, that he was unable to be aware of anything else but the task in hand.

He had bought the children time. Other than that, they were on their own.

* * *

Crematorium Hill was a killer, especially after the sprint across town, but Tom and Jazz didn't let up their pace until they were at the top and at the entrance to the grounds of Raingate Crematorium. There were no gates, just expanses of grass, crisscrossed by paths that were bordered by plaques bearing the names of people who had been cremated. The eeriness seeped into Tom's and Jazz's veins like acid, as blackening clouds stacked up overhead in the wind, obliterating the moon again. The clouds looked like a bizarre, sky-high audience, peering down and waiting for the show to start.

There, a hundred metres or so away on the other side of the grassed areas, stood the bleak-looking crematorium, with its chimney stack pointing to the skies, like a devilish finger.

Tom had no idea how long they stood panting on the edge of the grounds, but he suddenly became aware of Jazz looking at his phone. Her thumbs were dancing on the keys and she appeared completely absorbed – temporarily unaware that he was watching her.

"Jazz!" Tom hurried, "What are you doing?"

Jazz blinked quickly, sliding the phone shut and pushing it into her pocket; then she looked up at Tom. "Er, just checking the time," she hesitated, not convincing Tom at all. However, he had no time to consider his doubts as Jazz added: "We've got less than a minute to get there." 'There' was the Crematorium building itself, and before Tom had time to speak, Jazz began the final stretch of the sprint – straight across the grass, hurdling plaques and paths alike, heading for the structure that seemed to be waiting - a ghoul in the dark - for them to arrive. Tom did the instinctive thing and belted after her into the dark and the unknown.

Chapter 35

Inside.

In the dark.

A monster watches.

Chapter 36

They were neck and neck by the time they slammed into the wall. Tom felt more scared than ever before in his life. The bricks of the Crematorium wall felt cool beneath his fingers. He'd seen this building hundreds of times in his life, as he passed by it on the bus into Wakefield City Centre. But he could only remember seeing it during the day; in the daylight the Crematorium looked ... *well* ... ordinary. Even when its chimney smoked, there was nothing to fear about it. It was simply a place where people said goodbye to loved ones.

But tonight... The darkness smothered it like a vampire's cloak. Whatever moonlight there had been, was now gone; devoured by the ravenous clouds. Jazz squinted her eyes and tried to look everywhere at once, but eventually she gazed up, trying to distinguish the roofline from the sky. Everything merged together – blurring – as if the fabrics of the world were melting into one another.

A roar from the road signalled the passing of a large, fast motorbike. The growling engine loomed into their ears, causing them both to spin round in the shattered silence. They watched the glaring headlamp expand, till it reached a peak, then it diminished along with the howling engine, away into the distance. The light and sound of the motorbike winked out into nothing, to leave the blackness and the silence, along with the withering wind, as the children's only companions.

Or so they thought…

Something in the periphery of his vision made Tom turn slowly back to the ominous building. Jazz must have heard his quick gasp of shock because she spun around to follow his gaze. Over to their left, the large front entrance doors to the Crematorium were wide open. Someone – *something* – had opened them in the fleeting seconds it had taken the motorbike to pass by.

In the gloom, the entrance appeared a darker shade of black. Jazz thought it looked like a gullet, ready to swallow them up.

Chapter 37

They felt as if they were standing on the edge of a black, bottomless pit. They teetered there, knowing that great danger awaited within. They also knew that if they did not go on, they would probably never see Doc again.

Jazz grabbed Tom's wrist and pressed the 'light' button on his watch. Somewhere in the back of Tom's mind a nagging little question whispered: *Jazz had only just checked the time on Tom's mobile phone. Why was she checking again?* But of course, time was of the essence tonight. The little glowing screen on his wristwatch told them it was 11:40pm. Approximately twenty minutes before the Caveman's spell on Doc's family would wear off… Somehow, as if in a nightmare, the evening had whipped by in a flash. So quick – and so horrible.

Taking a deep breath, Tom took Jazz by the elbow. "Best get moving," he stated, in a hush that was barely a whisper.

They stepped across the threshold, into the dark.

Chapter 38

Without consciously realizing it, Tom and Jazz were holding hands by the time they were two or three steps into the belly of the Crematorium.

"Isn't that sweet?" An old-lady-voice pervaded the blackness. It wasn't familiar to the children, and its granny-soft texture seemed totally out of place. Jazz felt Tom squeeze her hand a little tighter and she felt better for it.

Their eyes – too slowly for comfort – were beginning to accustom themselves to the murk. Rows of low seats began to emerge in their vision, on either side of them like pews in a church. As things grew less gloomy, the interior of the building began to reveal itself; it looked a bit like a chapel. The pews on either side continued along the length of the place until they stopped, about thirty metres ahead, where a long platform - like a stage - rose up, accessible by three wooden steps.

The waft of open drains and dead things was strong in the air, making the children screw up their faces and feel sick. Tom thought he could make out a cabinet on the platform – then he realized it was a lectern; on top of it was a statue of an eagle with spread wings. And standing behind it…

"Come, children. Don't be shy." The elderly-woman-voice sang out again, but this time it didn't sound so sugary-nice; there was mockery in it. The voice was coming from a form that was all too familiar to them. It hovered, slightly above the ground, with tentacular whips of fiery hair.

The doors through which they had entered slammed shut.

Chapter 39

Tom and Jazz jumped out of their skins. They spun around in shock and saw the dreaded outlines of two scorpionesque guards, one on either side of the closed doors. They were trapped, like flies in a jar.

Fear held them like a gripping fist. The rotten smell began to change slightly. Another odour had joined it. Wood smoke. The origin of the new smell was unclear, until flames crept from the rear pews, feeding hungrily on the wood; small at first, but soon growing in intensity, illuminating the sinister faces of the hideous giant scorpions. They grinned malevolently, eyes like black grapes.

Soon the flames became a blaze – engulfing the rear pews on both sides. The two friends could feel the heat and they instinctively backed away from it, towards the raised platform where the fire-monster waited. Their retreat was made all the more quick as the second-to-back rows ignited and whooshed into flame.

"Get up here now! Or *he* gets it!" The old-lady-voice was positively evil now, as it shrieked the order. Simultaneously, the lights above the platform flickered on, to reveal the spine-chilling sight of Doc, captive in a cage. The cage dangled from the ceiling, approximately three metres above the floor. Doc appeared to be unconscious. Both Tom and Jazz hoped it was not any worse than that…

The beast allowed a few seconds to crawl by, in order to let the children absorb the full impact of their situation: the burning pews, the doors closed and guarded by monsters, and their best friend swinging gently to and fro from a hook, high above in the ceiling. And lastly, but by no means least, here was the hovering fire-monster, with crackling flames for hair, pinpoint red lasers in black pits for eyes, and needle teeth in her gash of a mouth.

She cackled; an evil, cheerless chuckle that ran Jazz's blood cold and made her take an involuntary step away. At this, the scorpion guards rattled and clattered, signalling 'no way out'.

Tom looked Jazz straight in the eye, "Come on, we'll be okay." Tom tried to sound reassuring, but he failed. His attempted smile trembled on his lips. Jazz understood and, mustering her courage, she took the first steps forward. Tom hastily followed, his mouth dry and his pulse pumping. The whole room danced and twisted with the crazy combination of electric light, leaping flames and writhing shadows.

They stepped up on to the raised platform together. Whatever happened, they would face it as a team. "Doc! You okay?" Jazz shouted, trying to sound as brave as she could, but feeling very scared. To her surprise, Doc stirred and groaned a little.

"He'll come round shortly," the creature-woman said. "I just gave him a little something to keep him quiet till you both arrived." The voice sounded wicked and sharp, like an evil old granny. "Quite a noisy little fellow. Made all sorts of threats to me, about what the two of you were going to do when you got here. So, how about it? Do you want to free your little friend?" She paused here, before adding: "The thing is, if you do try to release him, you might find yourself getting a little hot under the collar!" She snorted with crazy laughter at her own feeble joke, and the scorpion guards cackled along with her.

Jazz put on a brave front. "We just want you to get lost, actually."

Tom cringed as he wondered what the response of the monster-woman would be, but she simply replied very calmly and coldly: "Oh, that's just what I intend to do. I'll get lost where no one will ever find me. Maybe I'll take you with me..."

The smell of burning grew stronger and Tom heard more pews beginning to crackle. Whilst Jazz and the monster stared at each other, Tom glanced quickly at Doc's cage. He noticed that the base of it was a trapdoor, held fast only with a bolt, underneath; the bolt was well out of Doc's reach. But if Tom could get to it, at the right moment, then he might be able to slide it open and free Doc.

"And what about you, sonny boy?" the creature leered. "Are you feeling as stupid – er, brave – as your girlfriend, here?"

"I'm not his girlfriend!" Jazz snapped. This retort was met by a snarl and the flames on the creature's head flared menacingly, making Jazz step back behind Tom, in spite of herself.

Tom interjected swiftly, to try to stop this impossible quarrel getting out of hand. He had to buy them time. "Please may we sit down?" he asked and, receiving no refusal from the monster, he sat on the floor and gestured for Jazz to do the same. "Can I ask – what do you really want with us, Zeduza?" The name almost burned his lips.

A look of surprise came across the creature's sinister face. "So – you know my name?"

Nervous as he was, this was just what Tom had hoped for - to distract her, to try to think of some way out of this; though how they could possibly escape was beyond him at the moment. The only way out was barred by flames and giant scorpions. And worse still, nobody knew they were there.

"Yeah, and we know what you did too, you moron!" Jazz snapped again. Tom sometimes wished that Jazz had a zip on her mouth that he could pull across to keep her quiet. Deep down, though, he admired her guts. She certainly wasn't one to cower in a corner. But Tom also knew that if there was any hope at all, bravery wasn't enough, and brute force was out of the question. The only glimmer of hope they had was to keep the beast talking and somehow try to out-think her – if she let them live long enough.

"Please forgive my friend," Tom put in quickly, "She can be a bit sharp at times." At this, Jazz looked stunned and poked him with her elbow. "We do know what you did, but I don't understand why you can't just let us go now. You have the necklace back." He pointed at the pendant, which now nestled amongst the other weird trinkets on her strange costume.

A shuffling sound came from the cage. Tom and Jazz turned their heads to look. Doc had got himself into a sitting position. They had no idea how long he'd been conscious, but he was rubbing a hand back and forth over the top of his head. To Tom's surprise, Doc's eyes looked very clear and sharp, as if he'd been awake for ages. "Doc! What did she do to you?" Tom gasped, amazed.

"She made me take a pill, and wash it down with some weird green liquid," he pointed to a glass phial towards the rear of the staged area. "Problem – for her – was that I drank the drink, but…" He unfurled his right hand, and there in the palm was an oval-shaped yellow tablet. He risked a grin in the direction of the monster-woman.

Zeduza hissed and her eyes looked like thunder. Doc's grin dissolved like an ice-cube in a microwave. But he braced himself and carried on. "So, while she thought I was out for the count, I overhead some of what she was saying to the ugly bugs, over there." The scorpions growled angrily and started scuttling up the aisle towards him, but Zeduza raised a clawed hand and they retreated. Wow – Doc was on a roll. When he started talking, Jazz had nothing to match him. He could insult people for Britain! However, even Doc knew when enough was enough; he breathed a long sigh of relief that the guards hadn't mauled him and said, "The fact is, I heard her telling those two," another grumble from the scorpions, "that she was luring you here. Please tell me that you told someone, and that the cavalry is on the way…"

The huge wall of silence from Tom and Jazz was answer enough.

"So, nobody knows that we're here?" Doc ventured, eyes wide with concern. A loud pop made the three children jump, as the heat from the flames made a window on one of the side walls explode. Glass shattered outwards and wind rushed inwards, feeding the blaze even more.

"But," Tom reiterated, "I still don't understand why we're here. You got what you wanted, you got the horrible chain back."

Jazz's former bravado was burning away as surely as the raging pews, but she dared herself to ask: "Are you just going to kill us? Is that why you brought us here?"

Doc didn't give Zeduza a chance to reply. "No. At least not yet. She needs us for something."

"For what?" Tom said.

"I don't know. All I heard was that she needed you here; needed all of us here, together."

The saccharine granny voice oozed from the monster's lips again, "Oh dear, dear me, young Daniel. No good ever came from eavesdropping."

"Who have you nicked that voice from?" Doc said, with his usual tact. "We know how it's done because the Caveman - " He realized too late that he had revealed their greatest ally, the one who had helped them along the way, and given them important clues about the fiery creature. He closed his mouth, really rather obviously.

"Whoops – cat out of the bag, eh, young Daniel?" Zeduza drawled.

The boys exchanged glances; Tom was still trying and still failing to look reassuring, giving Doc that 'it doesn't matter, mate' kind of look.

"Oh, don't worry. I've known about him all along. You see, myself and your 'Caveman' friend exist in the same state. We are of the ether; ghosts, in a way, though not exactly. He cannot directly hurt me, nor I him. That's why he left the job to you. And you failed miserably," she chortled maliciously. "Of course, we have many powers, but we possess no physical body. I, however, intend to do something about that…"

A crash rang through the building as the back rows of pews collapsed. The heat was beginning to get most uncomfortable, but Zeduza seemed to revel in it, as did the armour-plated guards at the doors. Sweat trickled down Jazz's back; she noticed that Doc had manouevered himself into a kneeling position.

Tom braved the question. "So, you're going to take our bodies? Use them somehow for yourself, like a kind of Frankenstein monster?"

"No, no, no," the creature laughed derisorily. "All this adventure has melted your brain. I cannot inhabit your body, or anyone else's. I *shall* be taking back my own body."

Chapter 40

All voices fell silent. The wind whipped through the broken window, billowing drapes which caught alight. Doc's chain creaked eerily as it swung slightly in the gusts. The smell of smoke and decay clogged the air. Eventually, the monster-woman casually muttered: "Harriet Benson, by the way."

The name rang a bell in Tom's mind. Where had he heard it before?

"One of my neighbours from the graveyard? It's *her* cute little voice I'm using. *Relaxing, isn't it?*" The last three words combined with Zeduza's terrible trademark screech, and made the children cringe and cover their ears. Hands clasped to their heads, the three friends watched as the monster raised an arm and extended her claw-fingers to an area on the left. The children had not noticed this before; it was the most dimly lit place in the building. Then a rush of flame escaped Zeduza's fingers and the carpet woofed into flame, revealing a strangely beautiful scene. A porch-like entrance, built from white marble, was built into the wall. Extending from it, into the building itself, was a narrow plinth. It looked to Tom a bit like a shop counter, but it had a conveyor of some sort on top. Above the arch of the 'porch' an exquisitely carved angel, made from the same white marble, was shown in mid take-off, coming from the wall itself, as if to fly into the large room.

The children removed their hands from their ears. Zeduza still had her arm extended, as she said, "See the door beyond the little porch? That's where the furnace is. Can get mighty warm in there. Just like my lovely home planet. You know, the surface temperature on Sweltian-One would be enough to evaporate your blood…"

A fraction of a second later, the flame-creature flared up in brilliant white light and the whole room shook, as if a small earthquake had taken place. Semi-hypnotised, the children watched as her terrifying form began to alter. It became gaseous and whirled quickly, each part disengaging and mixing with the others in a cyclone of light and spectral matter. It reminded Tom of how the Tasmanian Devil looks in the cartoons, when he gets mad. The blisteringly hot air around the monster swirled outwards, filling their lungs and making it more difficult to breathe.

The tornado that was Zeduza gathered speed until the intensity of the sight was dazzling. Then in a great roar of sound and motion, the spinning shape shot towards Jazz, who sat open-jawed. Within an eye-blink, it had disappeared from sight, into Jazz's gaping mouth, down her throat, and into her eyes and ears.

Jazz jolted like she'd been hit by lightning, and sat up ramrod straight.

Tom's stomach lurched when he looked at her face.

Her eyes were black hollows, each with a wicked pinpoint of red light in the centre.

Chapter 41

The television flashed random lights around the room. The people were beginning to stir. Even though there was no outward sign, the Caveman was aware that their minds were starting to surface from the subconscious realm.

His power over them had been fully used. He was drained. Within moments they would open their eyes and assume they had simply dozed off.

When they did, the Caveman would be gone.

Chapter 42

"J-Jazz..?" Tom, still seated next to her, instinctively started to shuffle away, only stopping when he felt the edge of the platform. Jazz wasn't moving; she just sat upright, staring straight at him, with those terrible unearthly eyes that were set in Jazz's familiar face. The clothing of the monster was draped on her too, although it was ridiculously large on her small body. Chillingly, the shrunken heads, including the one best known to them, were strung around her upper body.

In the periphery of his vision, he could see that Doc was now standing upright in the gibbet-like cage. Tom made an almighty effort not to look; he didn't want to attract attention to Doc for the wrong reason. Then a most amazing thing happened: Jazz spoke. And the words that came out were spoken, not in some monstrous tone, but in Jazz's own, everyday voice.

"Tom – help me. I'm scared. You've got to help me, fast."

Tom was baffled. The being in front of him appeared to be a hybrid of Jazz and Zeduza. The facial features remained those of his friend, yet the eyes were other-worldly. The clothes were the creature's but the size of the body matched Jazz perfectly. The voice was Jazz's – or so he thought, until it spoke again. "Too late! No one can save her now!" came the wicked-old-lady voice. "She's mine for the taking!"

Then the Jazz-thing's form began to judder before settling still once more. Tom scrambled to his feet and, turning to Doc, he winced as another crack and bang suggested that yet another window had blasted out with the heat. "What do we do?!" Tom yelled in Doc's direction; the sounds of burning and destruction were getting louder. He saw Doc shake his head and point upwards, a look of intense alarm on his face. "We're all goners if we don't get out of here soon." Doc said hoarsely. Whether it was the heat and smoke that were hurting Doc's throat, making him rasp, Tom couldn't tell. Perhaps, he was on the verge of breaking down. When Tom swivelled his gaze up to see where Doc indicated, he was appalled to see the wooden beams of the roof ablaze.

"Tom! I can't hold her off much longer!" This was Jazz's voice again, coming from the hybrid. "If you're gonna save me, you have to do it now!"

Head swirling, Tom clutched his hair in his hands. "How?! Tell me, then!"

Jazz's voice erupted again, full of urgency and fear: "Free Doc from the cage, then you both have to come and join hands with me. A triangle of friendship! If we can work up enough positive energy, we might be strong enough to get her out of me. I don't think she can beat us if we stick together!" She managed to raise her strangely clawed hands in encouragement.

"Quick, Tom – do as she says!" Doc blasted, and Tom dashed across to the suspended cage. His fingers, wet with sweat, found it difficult to grasp the bolt beneath the cage and he hissed angrily under his breath, *"Come on, come on!!"* Finally he managed to grip the head of the bolt. With a titanic pull, he drew the bolt across, and the trapdoor base of the cage slammed down. Tom had to jump back swiftly, as Doc tumbled out like bowling ball and landed flat on his backside on the stage.

"Hurry up!" Jazz pleaded. Her hair was starting to smoulder.

The boys hurtled to the place where she sat and, without hesitation, Tom and Doc grasped one each of her hands. They completed the connection by grabbing hold of each other's free hand. It was one of the worst mistakes of their lives.

Chapter 43

"Come on, mate. Job's done."

"With you in a sec, Jack," replied Ted Allerton, wiping the back of a grimy hand across his forehead and leaning against the cool, steel side of the fire engine. His colleagues were beginning to scramble back into the vehicle. Ted had one last, long look at the blackened and dripping barn, to make sure there were no more sparks lingering around. The team had been called out to Shadwell's Farm, by old Mr Shadwell himself. The hay barn was already alight when the call was made, and the blaze was roaring away when their tyres skidded to a halt, a few minutes later; but the firemen had quickly got the blaze under control and had managed to keep the damage to a minimum. Farmer Shadwell said he'd seen some youths running away.

Ted shook his head as he climbed back into the driver's seat. He was glad that Tom was a good lad and kept himself out of trouble. As he prepared to start the engine, he felt something vibrate in his shirt pocket. His mobile. He took it out and peered at the screen: *One new text message.* No wonder he'd missed it – he had been fighting a fire for the last fifteen minutes! He pressed the 'view' button and read the text. Letting out a gasp, as if he'd been bitten by a snake, he let the phone drop to the floor of the cab and fired the ignition. The engine growled angrily as he stamped hard on the accelerator.

"Buckle up!" he commanded and, before his colleagues had a chance to ask where they were going, Ted Allerton's fire engine was skidding out of Shadwell's gate, wheels spinning and kicking up dirt.

Farmer Shadwell watched from his front door as the tail lights of the engine receded into the distance, like a pair of fiery eyes.

Chapter 44

Tom and Doc felt as if electrical currents were flowing through them. Not enough to cause them pain, but enough to immobilize them completely. Something had got inside of them, the instant they had joined hands with Jazz. And, though their bodies were stuck fast, their minds were sprinting.

What had happened? Why couldn't they move? What was Jazz doing to them?

A foul chuckle broke the chains of thought. The mirthless laughter came from the Jazz-hybrid. The monster had read their thoughts and had *felt* their pulses quicken. "Time is short." The voice that came from Jazz was the old-lady tone again; old-lady sprinkled with pure badness. "I have all the elements in place now, so I may as well tell you how this is going to work." Tom and Doc were mere puppets in her control. They were forced to listen.

"I know your guardian Caveman has told you all about my murky past. So you know who I'm wearing round my neck. As you can see, he wasn't the first," she smirked, glancing down at the string of shrunken skulls. "Hmm... Big brother Lakkesh tangled with the wrong sister when he tried to stop me from being Queen. Of course, once my loose-lipped bodyguards had let my little secret slip, they had to pay the price – and Daddy turned them into the *beautiful* creatures that they are today." The scorpions grated their massive claws against the ground. "Only problem was, I got punished too. Life can be so unfair at times…" Again she giggled like an insane infant.

Part of the roof collapsed over to their right, a few metres from the furnace area. The falling wood and masonry sounded like a weird round of applause. The Zeduza-Jazz looked up and saw a gaping orifice up in the rafters; high above that, in an inky sky, she saw the full moon glaring down, like an impatient eye. She hurried on: "The moment your little friend, Jazz, poked her nose into the tomb on Halloween, she set in motion a chain of events that have been waiting for millennia to happen - she unearthed the pendant. The moon and the starlight were the catalyst that I had been waiting for. They light the way to my own galaxy, to Swelt. And I shall *return* there, this very night. All thanks to you, children, of course."

Jazz felt herself waking. She wondered where she was; what was happening. She was rooted the spot, holding hands with Tom and Doc. *Why couldn't she move? And why could she hear the old-woman's voice in her head?*

"Oh, boys," Zeduza-Jazz crooned, "Your *girl*friend has joined us." The boys really wanted to get at this monster and hit her. So did Jazz. "You see," the crone-voice continued, "I have a little confession to make. Unless I could connect, *physically*, with the three of you, I could not have direct control over you. I have to admit, you gave me problems for a while. But once I used Daniel's phone to lure you over here, after dressing up the old man in the graveyard and getting the two

145

of you to give him a good soaking (he was rather easy to control of course, once I got inside him), you played right into my hands. Taking Daniel and bringing him here was child's play. I mesmerized him just like I mesmerized Jasmine on the first night we met. And when *Jazz* pleaded with you to come and hold her hands… well… it wasn't really Jazz. It was me…"

The boys realized then just how hopeless their situation was. The monster had used Jazz's voice just like she had used the old lady's. Once she had got inside Jazz it had been easy. Doc silently cursed himself for being so gullible; not only had she snatched him from the graveyard, but he'd fallen for this trick as well.

"And once the connection was made – I had you; stuck, like pins on a magnet!" The heat was almost unbearable for the children now. Most of the pews had ignited, windows shattered and rafters splintered. Sweat ran down their backs.

"Once my father had jettisoned me from our planet, in that prison of rock, he thought I was doomed. And I would have been too, if I hadn't used the power of the pendant to my own advantage. I *poured* all my energy, all my *life-force*, into it. I *became* the pendant; protected by bone and metal. Fractions of an Earth-second before crashing to the ground and crushing your Caveman friend, I discharged my physical body. It wasn't easy, but there was a weak point in the structure of the rock. By the power of the pendant, I *willed* my body out, through the surface of the rock. My body grounded nearby, but the *essence* of me was in the pendant." Whilst the monster could read the children's thoughts, they too could sense the pleasure, the ecstasy that Zeduza was getting from finally being able to tell her tale, to this truly captive audience.

"Millions of your Earth years later, Raingate Cemetery was built on top. And I have waited all this time for someone like you to come along…"

A thought gnawed at Tom's mind: *Why did she eject her body? She would never have any hope of retrieving it. And yet, earlier she had hinted at regaining her physical form…*

Zeduza picked up on the thought. "Of course I can retrieve my body; well, *my bones.* Even though they might be a bit fossilized." The idea amused her and she chuckled again. "Because, children, even my very bones have power. They are lying in wait for me to reunite, to take them home and have my revenge. It was no accident that your kings built a castle on top of my remains, now was it? *Sandal* Castle, I believe you call it. It has protected my bones for the last part of my waiting."

A ground-shuddering thud rang out, as a large section of the wall to the left cracked and toppled in.

Zeduza breathed deeply through Jazz's lungs, enjoying the taste of the smoke and the searing heat. Jazz just wanted to scream – but she couldn't. "So now, the jigsaw is complete. The power of the pendant is peaking, the pull of the full moon is at its height, and the conjoined energy that comes from your friendship is stronger than all the rest combined."

The boys felt themselves being *turned* against their wills, so that

147

they all faced the entrance doors. Instinctively, the scorpion guards scuttled away to the sides, as the doors flew inwards with a mighty crash, and wind rushed in to fan the already ravenous flames.

Tom and Doc could see outside again – and their hearts sank, as they knew there was no chance of getting there. The full moon and flames bathed everything in a strange luminescence; the Crematorium grounds, the road, and Pugney's Lake in the distance. Sitting in front of, and partially obscuring the lake, was the monstrous motte of Sandal Castle.

"Time for the reunion!" the monster announced.

And to the children's further horror, they saw the mound of the castle begin to pulse and bulge. Even from this distance, the metamorphosis from a simple large hill was obvious. The motte was re-forming itself, into something twisted and terrible. When they saw what it was, the children felt the last embers of hope die out.

Chapter 45

The Caveman had left the house. The occupants were beginning to stir.

He felt drained, his powers dulled by the extended period spent subduing Doc's family. He had hoped that it would have given the children time enough to return the necklace and get back home. He sensed that neither of these things had happened.

The message that emblazoned itself on his thoughts was: *Danger. Great danger.*

He sensed intense heat; awesome power. And he knew that Zeduza was close to victory.

Chapter 46

Zeduza had inverted the triangle, so that now the boys faced the open doors. She herself did not need Jazz's eyes to see; even though the girl was facing the back of the building, the occurrence was projected into the monster's mind's-eye.

In the distance, the large mound that still held the relics of Sandal Castle, alternately expanded, then contracted; almost as if it were breathing. The black silhouette of its outline slowly changed colour. It appeared as though it were being *lit* from the inside, from the centre. It glowed firstly a dull red, then intensified with each passing moment until it went through crimson, orange and now a vivid and harsh yellow, so bright that it hurt the boys' eyes to watch.

But watch they did, and as the mound began to stop its pulsating, and the yellow glare formed a ghostly halo around the edges, two large dark patches grew from the epicentre. In the exact centre of *these* appeared two dazzling compressions of red laser light. With terrifying speed the remainder of Zeduza's image burned itself on to the motte, until a giant face glowered back at them.

A violent rumble resonated from overhead, as a car-sized chunk of roof gave way and plummeted down towards the children. This large lump broke into several smaller pieces as it descended. The bits of roof landed like shrapnel, close by to where the group sat immobilized. One piece glanced off Tom's shoulder, making a small rip in his coat and sending a sharp message of pain to his brain. Others bounced harmlessly onto the staged area – but one fist-sized fragment, however, struck Jazz's left arm, just below the elbow; the force of the blow caused her hand to break free of Doc's hand. With lightning recognition, Doc realized that fate had thrown them a chance: the connection had been broken. Just as quickly, Zeduza reached out to grab Doc's hand once more and rejoin the chain that held them fast. But Doc was already reaching inside his coat. With a flurry of movement and a look of triumph in his eyes, he withdrew from his large inside pocket, a water pistol – and it was fully loaded.

Without hesitation he pointed the gun straight into Jazz-Zeduza's face and squeezed the trigger hard. A thick, powerful jet of water sluiced into her face, drenching the features. He pumped at the trigger to keep the flow going and Zeduza released an ear-splitting screech of anger. Before the stream of water had run dry, Zeduza had exited Jazz's body, via her mouth, in a gaseous cloud of speeding matter, to form once more at the rear of the platform.

Tom had scrambled to his feet and Doc, the pistol now empty, threw the gun to one side and quickly stood up too. The pair of them grabbed Jazz's arms and hauled her to her feet.

Free of Zeduza's influence, they stumbled swiftly down the steps. Once back in the main aisle, they faced an impossible decision: Either they went back up, and faced the wrath of a seething Zeduza, or they went forward, to run the gauntlet of blazing pews and the hideous scorpion guards, that now reared and bucked in the open doorway.

"Let's turn up the heat a little," the wicked-old-lady voice said, and from the place where they had seen the stone angel earlier, a click and a huge boom of noise swelled out. The friends turned to see that Zeduza had moved over to the place where the porch led to the furnace. A colossal tower of flame rose up, devouring both the white angel and Zeduza in its wake. The sheer physical blast of the heat forced the children away down the central aisle and, dodging debris and dripping flames, the threesome dashed towards the exit and the ambush of the scorpion guards.

Chapter 47

Twenty metres from the gaping double doors, the children stopped, as Tom grasped his friends' arms and pulled them back. Red-faced from the intense heat, Jazz yelled, "Tom, what are you doing? We have to get past them!"

"It's our only chance, Tom. We have to risk the scorpions," Doc added, with urgency in his voice.

"Agreed," Tom said, surprisingly calmly.

"So, what are we waiting for?" Jazz insisted, and Tom thought he saw a flash of red in her eyes, but dismissed it as a reflection of the blaze.

"Jazz, you've just been possessed by that thing," Tom swept a hand towards where Zeduza had been. "And you Doc, you've been swinging in a cage, then saved the day by splatting Jazz in the face with water."

Doc shot a glance at Jazz, "Yeah, sorry about that."

Jazz just shook her head and looked again at Tom. "So?" she pressed.

"So… I'll take care of the scorpion guards. Then you two follow me. If my plan works, we'll be out of here in a few seconds."

"And if it doesn't work?" Doc queried, his face aghast.

Tom didn't reply, he just turned and ran full-throttle at the guards, which waited either side of the doors, as if goading him to try to get through before they closed in.

Chapter 48

The fire engine streaked through the back lanes and out on to the main road. The communications radio in the cab blared out an instruction for the fire crew: *Proceed directly to Raingate Crematorium. Nearby residents have reported a big blaze in the Crematorium buildings.*

Jack Murray slammed the blue lights on and set the sirens wailing. "Ted," he shouted over the clamour, "We've got to get to the Crem! Where were you headed for anyway?"

Ted Allerton gripped the steering wheel harder and hissed through clenched teeth: "Crem."

Jack looked across at him, nonplussed, then turned his gaze to the gathering orange glow, away in the distance at Raingate Crematorium.

Chapter 49

Jazz and Doc stood, dumbstruck, as Tom pelted along the treacherous aisle, dodging sections of burning pew and sidestepping slabs of hot masonry and glowing timber. He'd left them no option but to stand and watch, so quickly had his decision been made.

The demonic guards waited a few metres to each side of Tom's intended exit; their shiny black legs were braced and ready to pounce, their huge, lethal front claws were snapping closed and swishing open, over and over again, with a bone-clattering sound. Life seemed to run temporarily in slow motion, and Tom took in all this in micro-seconds – but worst of all, were the expressions on their obscenely human faces: they were *salivating* with anticipation at chopping him down.

In his dream-speed run, he closed the ground between himself and the poised-to-attack scorpions. With flames threatening to scorch him and smoke stinging his watering eyes, Tom found his way barred by a three-metre long beam of burning oak which, if it had fallen from the roof a split-second later, would have crashed down onto his head.

"Tom, get back!" Doc hollered, fearing that his friend would go headlong into the blazing beam.

Whether Tom had heard him or not, it was too late for him to stop so, acting purely on instinct, he bounced hard onto his front foot and hurdled over the red hot obstacle; he felt the heat on his thighs as he sailed over it, and his trailing foot scraped the crackling surface of the wood as he cleared it, hitting the ground on the other side with safety. Simultaneously, the guards rushed at him diagonally, closing off the width of the exit and the distance between themselves and their target.

They intended to either crush him between their mighty armoured bulks, or lop off his head with their slashing pincers - or both. With savage claws raised, they made the final pounce – but Tom wasn't there anymore. At the last possible moment, he threw his body forward and downwards and dived, headfirst to the floor. He scattered cinders and rubble as he went, miraculously avoiding being burnt. The scorpions became victims of their own vigorous momentum and, instead of hitting Tom, they collided with each other. With a noise like two large coconuts cracking together, they head-butted one another and, as Tom skidded clear on his belly, they somersaulted in mid-air and came crashing to the ground. They each gave a huge quiver and sank into unconsciousness, the knock-out blow being instantaneous.

Tom scrabbled to his feet and turned to see Jazz and Doc looking shocked in the chaos of flame and smoke. He waved an arm, gesturing them to him, yelling, "Well, come on then! Don't hang about there all day!"

Cheering like maniacs, Tom's friends wasted no further time, and set off after him, towards the now unguarded doorway and the sweet, fresh air beyond.

Chapter 50

Clambering over the conked-out scorpion guards was probably more scary than weaving through the burning building, but within a matter of seconds, Jazz and Doc had rejoined Tom, and they didn't stop running until they had reached the outer edge of the grounds. Tom's plan of getting past the guards had worked - or he'd got lucky - but that was the extent of it. Now, there was no plan. On the one side there was the leering face of the creature, glowing from the motte of the ruined castle. On the other, there was the real thing, raging and ready to pursue at any moment. No one had firm ideas about what to do next. So regaining their breath and refilling their aching lungs with cleansing air, after the muck of the Crematorium, seemed like a logical step.

The three of them collapsed to the ground onto the moist grass that verged the pavement and the road beyond. A distant siren, faint but gradually intensifying, prompted Doc to suggest, "I think we should call the police. She's gonna be after us any time now." He tapped his pockets. "Oh no, she's got my mobile!"

"Jazz, you've got mine. Ring the police, quick!"

Jazz nodded her agreement urgently, reaching into her pocket and yanking out Tom's mobile. She stabbed the emergency numbers on the keypad and held the phone to her ear. A man's voice on the other end asked: "Emergency – which service do you require?"

"Police. I need the police. Quickly. Please!"

"One moment please," the deep voice said, reassuringly.

Jazz gripped the phone like a lifeline, as they all sat watching the burning building, hawk-like, looking for any sign of the reawakening guards or the clawed monster woman.

Jazz hissed under her breath, "Come on, come on!" into the mobile phone speaker.

Desperate seconds passed, then a voice in the ear-piece broke the silence. "Yes, dear? How can I help?"

Jazz held the phone away from her ear, staring at it as if it had transformed into something hideous. "Oh, no…" were the only two words she could muster.

Doc gawped at her: "What's up, Jazz. Hey, come on, you're doing my head in."

Tom snatched the mobile unceremoniously from Jazz, who still sat gazing at her hand where the phone had been, as Tom put the unit to his own ear. "Hello, m'dear. It's only me… Your worst nightmare!" The soothing old-lady voice morphed into a vicious screech on those last three words. Tom dropped the phone like it was a red hot iron bar and it bounced onto the grass. Even though the mobile was not on speakerphone, the children were able to hear the wicked voice scream out its few remaining words: "Now watch and learn!"

Then the mobile burst into flames and proceeded to melt and crackle before their astonished eyes. It soon became apparent, however, as scary as that was, that this was not the main event that the creature wanted them to witness. A cacophonous howl broke from the fast collapsing Crematorium building, and the children raised their reddened eyes to look.

Chapter 51

A vast hole had opened up in the roof, as if it had been punched through by a giant fist. Smoke and flame billowed out and up from it. And from within this confusion, rose up an inferno of white, yellow and bright orange heat: a firestorm rising. This angry, towering furnace seemed to scrape the sky. To the children's terror, a figure began to form within this seething fortress. A weirdly holographic image of Zeduza swirled into existence and took up substance there, in the impossible heat. The boiling tower stood fifty metres high, and dazzled the children so that they had to shield their eyes and look away. Doing so revealed in graphic detail what the creature had prophesied: Zeduza was reclaiming her physical form.

The evil face in the motte dissembled, like ripples in an orange lake. The hill still emitted the glaring yellow-orange colours, but now the body of the mound began to *bubble*. It looked like it was starting to boil. Or to erupt. No sooner had the thought crossed Jazz's mind than the surface of the motte burst and *something* spewed out into the air. This was immediately followed by another explosion, as another unknown object was propelled from a different point on the hill. Another, then another and another blackened object ejected from various sections of the ravaged mound. It was as if the motte itself were vomiting, trying to rid itself of some long-held poison.

The dark, ancient artefacts spun around in the cold air of the dead hours, heading straight towards them. As the motte of the castle gave one last death-tremble, the feverish glow faded from it, and the entire mound collapsed in on itself, with a thunderous crash.

The darkling contents of the motte passed over the children's heads, at an almost leisurely pace; a skull, a skeletal foot, a femur, a ribcage, closely trailed by others of a similar kind.

These were the mouldering bones of Zeduza - and they journeyed, like guided missiles, into the heart of the towering inferno.

Chapter 52

An ear-aching discord of noise ripped out from the tower of heat, as the last of the bones flew in. The sound was a mixture of screeching, screaming and howling; the terrible cacophony of a demon choir in victory.

The children were trapped like rabbits in headlights, as the monster bellowed in triumph. The ferocity of the sound made their heads quiver and seemed to make the Earth itself shake.

Then a different sound joined this chaos. It came from behind them, getting closer... closer... closer. As they twisted their heads to look, this second monster loomed into view over the crest of the rise in the road. Growling, howling and red, with bright, piercing eyes, it sped towards them, as if to crush them in its wake.

The children closed their eyes and waited for the impact.

They felt the huge mass of the beast quaking the ground beneath them, and then it whooshed past them! Tom dared to open his eyes, and shouted out loud in relief; a sound that was part cheer, part sob.

The fire engine thundered off the road, onto the grass, and over the Crematorium grounds, closing the distance between itself and the conflagration in an instant. The crew leapt from the engine as it slewed to a halt, Ted Allerton looking back towards Tom and his friends. Tom raised a hand, as if to indicate he was okay, and his dad acknowledged the gesture, before returning quickly to the crew, and the bizarre fire that awaited them.

The team acted as one well-drilled body, the massive hose was unravelled, the powerful pumping mechanism was activated and, frighteningly quickly, the violent torrent of icy water cannoned out of the nozzle. The freezing blast impacted immediately, in a huge arc, upon the shimmering figure of the giant creature, which now let out a new cry; a mixture of anger and, perhaps, even fear. As the water hammered against the roof of the Crematorium and the base of the tower of flame, the massive flare began to gyrate in confusion and uncertainty. The fiery figure spiralled like a spinning top and twisted like a snake.

The children clapped their hands and cheered the firefighters on, as the monster writhed in the watery jets. Zeduza's plans had been halted in their tracks by the one thing she was unable to fight – the wet and the cold.

The titanic struggle between the monster-colossus and the brave fire crew raged for countless minutes, as the children yelled their encouragement. They felt their hearts rise, as the inferno began to diminish, only slightly - but certainly - getting smaller, as Zeduza's resistance was starting to weaken.

The children were not aware of the presence of the ghostly white Caveman fading away behind them and, such was the maelstrom of noise, nor could they hear the words of the fireman who called out from the engine, to Ted and the other crew: "We need back up, fast.

The tank's almost empty and there aren't any hydrants nearby!"

"How long?!" Tom's dad hollered over the thunder.

The reply was the last thing he wanted to hear. "Two more minutes – maximum. Then we're as dry as a bone."

Chapter 53

The surface of Pugney's Lake stippled in the gusting wind of the chill November night. The great white disc of the full moon was reflected in countless miniature images, as the water danced and buffeted. A cluster of sailing boats, moored at the far side, bobbed up and down, as if seeking attention from the tall figure that stood on the near bank in the shadow of a flailing willow.

The figure was old. Very old. But physically strong. His deeply-bronzed skin, cracked and flaky in places, covered powerful muscles. Had the whim taken him, he would easily have been able to tear the willow up by its roots. Yet his shoulders were slouched forward. He looked tired; mentally weary. Red-streaked eyes peered out from sunken sockets, as his hair blew wildly in the wind.

His spiritual energy was at a low ebb. The act of incapacitating Doc's family had left him almost drained. It would be hours before he fully recharged. And now he had to call on his powers again – or, at least what remained of them.

* * *

The cobra-like hose stuttered and shook, then lurched in the strong hands of the firemen.

"That's it – no more water left in the tank," Dave Denby called to his crew mates.

"How long till back-up arrives?" rasped Ted Allerton.

Jack Murray leaned out of the cab, where he was manning the radio, and shouted, "Should be here in about five minutes!"

By then, the whole place could be down – and whatever that thing is in the middle… Ted's thought trailed off in his mind as he peered up at the orange-red colossus that screamed in anger. Zeduza had been weakened by the onslaught of the firemen, but now that the water supply had been exhausted, she began slowly regathering her strength.

* * *

The Caveman's eyes once more burned a fiery red. Sweat beaded on his rough old flesh. He had drawn himself up to his fullest, most powerful height. Mustering all his strength and drawing on energy reserves that he knew could prove fatal were he to use them up, he raised his arms high, like a conductor in front of a huge liquid orchestra.

The gently chopping waters of the lake became more agitated, as if in response. Whirlpools – small at first – began swirling around in random patterns on the surface. Then explosions, like small bombs being triggered, erupted from the water.

The Caveman threw his head back and clenched his huge fists, till the knuckle bones nearly popped through. The wind howled and whipped anew, making trees and boats tremble and jump. He let out an almighty roar and, spectacularly, the far end of the lake began to curl up, like the beginnings of a wave. The chill lake water continued its rolling motion, rising up and leaving the gritty bed upon which it had lain for decades.

Up and up it rose, like a kite beginning to fly – and the whole of the lake seemed to morph into one weird, living mass. Like a tidal wave, the water lifted, flipped and towered, until the entire body of water spiralled up like a whirlwind with its base at the near bank, by the Caveman's pulsing form. Gravity was defied, the laws of physics were denied, as the mass of liquid gyrated there, as if waiting for a command from the timeless man.

With a vigorous movement, the Caveman pivoted on his heels and twisted his body to face away from the giant corkscrew of icy water. He then thrust out his arms, gnarled old fingers stretching out towards the haloed orange blaze that raged in the distance, at Raingate Crematorium. The massive volume of water arced over his head, whilst remaining anchored in the lake bed, with its free end slicing through the cold night air, like a slick knife, heading with intense velocity towards the Zeduza-fire.

Like a snake from Hell, it whiplashed over Sandal Castle, spearing straight for the Crematorium, and the boiling heart of Zeduza.

* * *

Zeduza was soaring higher once more, emitting a terrible stream of heat and light that caused the fire crew to back away, shielding their eyes with their arms. The fire-creature spotted the watery phenomenon coursing through the air and, at first, was unable to identify it. The glistening projectile resembled a shooting star, on a trajectory that would bring a collision course with Zeduza herself. But, as the unidentified flying object drew nearer, the monster realized that this was no star, and its vapour trail was not heat. The surging mass was aqueous – and it was on the attack. As the massive arc of water homed in on its fiery target, threatening to obliterate, Zeduza raised a mighty clawed hand and – palm first – met the icy onslaught.

The firemen were too close to see; their eyes were dazzled by the fierce light of the inferno. But as the three children squinted, they saw with intense clarity from their vantage point on the edge of the grounds. The thunderous snake of water battered against the upturned palm of Zeduza; a huge water cannon trying to break down her defences.

Zeduza howled in rage, fear and confusion as the water - seemingly with a life of its own - continued to hammer against her. Its descending curve was slowly but surely pushing her down.

The children were transfixed by a mixture of grim fascination and desperate hope. Zeduza was being ground lower and lower towards the ruins of the Crematorium – her spectral figure shrinking a little bit more with each second that passed.

"Go on!" Tom yelled.

Doc punched the air, shouting encouragement to their mysterious watery ally.

Jazz remained silent; just staring, staring …

Just when hope began to peak, however, Zeduza redoubled her efforts and began to turn the tide, in this titanic trial of strength. The high-pitched screech that surged out from her illustrated the energy that she was expelling, in order to drive the water back. And, to the children's horror, Zeduza rose skyward again - the firestorm excelsior - as the watery saviour was forced back.

* * *

The Caveman emitted a low, guttural moan, his strength sapping fast as he sank to his knees. His arms were still upraised, directing the gargantuan torrent towards its mark, but his energy was almost gone. Though his resolve and courage were as sure as ever, his power was fading and, with each moment that passed, he was driven further back.

He felt hollow with fatigue. His old bones ached. With one last brave surge, he pressed back with all his ancient might, but Zeduza was too strong. The Caveman was lifted from his feet and he slapped down, back first, in the gloopy mush of the lake bed. His broken form submerged, being quickly consumed by the sucking mud that drew him in like a sticky shroud. Within seconds he had gone – and the dark, deadly belly of the lake settled once more.

Zeduza had beaten him.

Chapter 54

The atmosphere crackled with static electricity. Zeduza has ceased her ear-blasting screeching. The horizontal column of water hung in the air, unmoving, like a strange bridge linking Pugney's and the Crematorium. All had fallen weirdly quiet.

The children took short, nervous breaths. The fire crew had backed away to a bearable distance and peered through narrowed eyes. Everything was gripped in expectancy. Ted Allerton ran over the grass, covering the distance between himself and his son within seconds. Tom stood up and leapt into his dad's arms, and the pair hugged each other like there was no tomorrow.

"You okay?" Dad gasped, sounding choked.

Tom just nodded, his face buried in Dad's shoulder. As Ted Allerton lowered his son to the ground to check him over and assess the damage to the other two, they were all distracted by a noise which broke the silence in the air above.

All eyes swivelled upwards to the barrage of water. It was moving again; the brief period of quiet was clearly over. The great rushing sound mimicked a hundred waterfalls, but none of the water came down. And none of the water went forwards.

"Dad … It's going backwards …" Tom spoke the words hesitantly.

"No! No!!" yelled Doc. "It's going the wrong way! Stop!"

Jazz just stared, impassively; not at the roaring water. She was staring at Zeduza. "Look …" she said quietly, pointing her finger at the burning column that was the fire-monster.

They all turned their attention in that direction - and jaws hung open in desperation. Zeduza now dominated the night like a skyscraper. She burned with a coppery incandescence; the intensity and brilliance of the light and heat now scorched the surrounding land, grass flaring up like dry straw. The Crematorium itself crumbled fast and collapsed like a condemned building that had been detonated.

Seeing the encroaching flames coming across the grass, the fire crew turned and fled towards the relative safety of the roadside. This instinctive action saved their lives, at least for the time being. The ravenous blaze engulfed the fire engine, like a nest of caustic snakes. The children heard the flames take hold, with a wild whoosh. Tom's dad grabbed him and, whilst barking out the order to *get down*, he bundled his son to the ground and placed his own body on top to shield him. The others threw themselves to the dewy grass and covered their heads as best they could.

A sonic boom tore the night apart as the fire engine exploded. Hundreds of litres of fuel ignited, blowing the vehicle apart like a giant tin can.

"Keep down!" yelled Dad, as the debris of the riven truck hurtled through the air and hammered to the ground in random disorder. Bits of engine bounced and clattered on the road, whilst other metallic chunks thumped wetly into the grass. A tyre rolled crazily past the vulnerable group as they huddled like rabbits. It bowled along, away onto the road and over the other side, where it came to rest in a cluster of bushes.

Andy Jameson, one of the younger firemen let out a yelp as a sliver of hot pipe from the fire truck's undercarriage, struck his lower leg, leaving a nasty gash in its wake. When the rain of boiling steel had finally subsided, Jack Murray scrambled across and began tending to Andy's wound.

Daring now to raise their heads again, the children and the fire crew looked across to where Zeduza loomed. She chuckled – a deep and throaty rasp that grated on their ears and made them cringe. Then she spoke, in a voice that was now like the screech of rusty hinges on an ancient door.

"Victory is mine. Despite the best efforts of the three of you," she gestured to the children with a sweep of a huge blazing hand. "I have prevailed. The process is complete. The old one's magic was useless against me." She paused to let out a wicked laugh, as the children absorbed the meaning of what she said: The Caveman had created the water cannon, but she had been stronger and driven him back. "Now, I shall return to my home galaxy and my own planet! I shall take what is rightfully mine – and rip the throne of the Sweltian from its present occupant. *I shall be Queen!!*"

To his dad's shock, Tom scrambled to his feet. "That's not rightfully yours! You're a murdering, thieving old witch!"

"Tom!" Dad yelled, as he tried to quieten his son, but now Doc was on his feet too.

"It's true, Mr Allerton! She's evil. She even killed her own brother! Now she's going back to start all over again – and she's stronger than ever." Doc's face was screwed up in anger.

Zeduza stopped laughing and pointed a finger of fire at the boys. "You," she hissed, "are impudent. You and that girl have meddled in things that are beyond your comprehension. You are no more than ants in the dust to me. And you will pay a heavy price for your interference."

An uneasy pause hung in the air before Zeduza spoke again. Tom and Doc remained standing, shaking with fear, but defiant. Tom's dad wrapped an arm round each boy's shoulders.

"Prepare to say goodbye to your irritating offspring," Zeduza directed this comment at Dad. "I'll be taking him and the other two with me now. By tomorrow they will be trinkets hanging from my belts; or, at least, their heads will." No more dramatic laughter came from Zeduza. She spoke with icy clarity from her immensity of flame and scorching heat.

"Time to go," Zeduza declared, and the mountain of heat began striding forward on legs that were pillars fire.

Tom's dad took a step forward but was driven back by the heat. The assembled group tried to run, but their legs would not respond. Zeduza had them in her grip, and was ready to take her trophies.

"No – get back!" Doc screamed.

174

"Leave us alone!" Tom yelled, knowing it was futile to protest.

"Take them and you'll have to go through me first!" Dad stood his ground, with all the power of a fly trapped in a giant spider's web.

"That'll do nicely ..." Zeduza intoned, in her evil croak, as she continued to advance.

Tom and Doc felt their faces begin to scorch, and turned their heads away in despair. As they did, Doc's gaze alighted on Jazz, who still sat calmly on the verge, as if in some kind of trance. He gave a gasp, like he'd seen a ghost, and tugged on Tom's sleeve.

"Tom," he said. *"Look at her eyes!"*

Chapter 55

Jazz looked out on to the alien planet. In the half-light she saw the skeletal, wizened trees. Instead of leaves, they bore shrunken skulls of whitish yellow which clacked together in the deathly breeze, like terrible wind-chimes. Further ahead, she made out other sounds, similar to these; the new clattering noises were being made by scorpions bearing human-like faces that emerged from the dusk.

Her eyes searched for the heinous creature of flame that she knew would not be far away. Strain as she did, she was unable to witness its presence. But she knew it was there; it was so close she could smell its rotting-meat stench.

Puzzled, she raised her hand to scratch her head. Her hand was smouldering and each long finger ended in a talon. The hand burst into flame and lit up the immediate area around her. To her horror, she saw that she was floating several metres above the ground, and the shadow that she cast had hair that writhed like a battalion of snakes.

Her eyes snapped open and she became aware of her place in the present – the here and now - once more.

The scene that surrounded her was chaotic; a maelstrom of light, heat and fear.

"Look at her eyes!" she heard Doc yell.

Tom turned his face to see. Jazz's eyes had become dark pits of nothingness, each centred only by a pinpoint of red laser light. She slowly got to her feet, and Tom couldn't quite shake the illusion that she was somehow *floating* just above the grass.

Simultaneously, Zeduza stopped dead in her tracks.

Jazz stared hard at the approaching colossus, and their laser eyes met. "I can smell your fear, Zeduza," Jazz said, matter-of-factly.

"What are you?" the giant tilted her head on one side, with curiosity.

"You're about to find out …" Jazz replied calmly, and she turned her eyes up to the still-retreating horizontal column of water. The monster seemed nonplussed, at a complete loss as to what was going on. Suddenly, the massive bridge of water reversed once more and began barrelling towards the flaming giant. Zeduza raised a palm again, to meet the force of the oncoming water; but this time she staggered back, and everyone heard her let out a huge gasp of shock and exertion.

Jazz raised her hands, in exactly the same way the Caveman had done, and with a flourish, drove the water on at even greater velocity. Zeduza howled and stumbled back yet again. Jazz thrust her arms forward again, and this time Zeduza sank to her blazing knees. Furthermore, to the amazement of the onlookers, her form began to *shrink*; only slightly at first, but more noticeably with every passing second.

"You might have beaten our brave Caveman," Jazz shouted above the clamour, "but he weakened you, didn't he? You're just bluff and bluster! There's nothing much left for you to give. Have some of your own medicine!" And with that, the force of the water increased tenfold, dowsing and shrinking and reducing the awful fire-menace with every heartbeat.

Zeduza emitted new sounds now; a mixture of pitiful pleas for mercy, and bone-chilling curses that swore revenge. She was already reduced to the size of a normal adult, by the time she barked the words: "A curse be on you all! I shall return to wreak my revenge, unless you release me now!"

"No way!" Jazz vociferated in response, and the might of the water continued to erode Zeduza's war-like body.

Zeduza gave a terrifying screech at this refusal and her body transformed itself from the shape that they all knew, to nothing more than a floating orange ball, like a miniature sun. This weird sphere hung in the air, crackling and fizzing, emitting bright sparks of orange, yellow and blue. Still, Jazz persisted with the onslaught of the water. She was unstoppable!

The flaming globe juddered and vibrated at an incredible speed. Then it exploded. Hundreds of round black objects, like ebony bullets, fired out in all directions, striking the onlookers on heads, bodies, arms and legs. They cried out in pain as the wicked little projectiles pelted them. Only Jazz seemed impervious to the peppering. She stood her ground, as the pellets that had gone upwards splattered down like black rain, some hitting the road and pavement, some hitting humans, some bashing into the soft earth and becoming buried there. The velocity of the explosion meant that the strange bullets had covered a radius of several hundred metres in all directions.

It was Jazz's turn to give a cry of triumph, as the fiery ball now *imploded* and dropped a cargo of mouldering bones to the ground, before fizzling away into nothingness.

All that could be heard was a fading cry of anger from Zeduza, drifting away on the wind, into the atmosphere.

Jazz moaned gently and crumpled to the ground. Tom's dad rushed over to her and raised one of her eyelids; as he did so, both Tom and Doc saw that the eye looked completely normal once more.

"She's fainted," Dad said, and set about putting her in the recovery position.

A gentle drizzle began to fall from the sky and, in the distance, the sirens of the back-up fire engines could be heard rushing to the scene of the devastated Crematorium.

A few metres away from where Tom and Doc watched Dad give first aid to Jazz, a smouldering set of bones hissed quietly in the misty rain. Zeduza's disassembled skeleton lay heaped up; a harmless stack of bones. In its midst, catching the glint of the moon, were hints of golden chain attached to smaller chunks of bone, that stared eyelessly into the night.

Chapter 56

The area was a mass of activity. A melee of flashing blue lights, police cars, fire engines and an ambulance combined with hurried conversations, men and women rushing hither and thither and a rainstorm that now lashed down like a monsoon.

"Could have done with this lot half an hour ago!" Doc heard one of the firemen call to a colleague. Doc was wrapped in a blanket and sitting next to Tom, comfortable in the back seat of a car. They'd both stopped shivering from the cold and the fright and were sipping hot chocolate that Mrs Studd had brought in a flask, out of plastic cups. As soon as the area had been made relatively safe, Tom's dad had contacted Mum and then got in touch with both Doc's and Jazz's parents, the latter of whom had taken some reaching, having been at a conference for the evening. Mr and Mrs Baxter had then gone off with Jazz in the ambulance. The medics reassured them and the boys that she was just being taken in for observation because of her fainting, and they needed to do some precautionary tests.

The boys' parents were all standing under a temporary gazebo that had been put up by the police. They were talking animatedly, and the boys knew that there would be some serious explaining to do; but that would come after much needed hot baths and a night's sleep. Mr Allerton had also told them that the police would want to talk to them to try to find out what on Earth had gone on.

What on Earth ... Tom had thought when Dad had said it, that Earth would probably not be the most relevant location in the retelling of events. And he had looked up to the murky sky where the moon had once more run and hidden.

Doc let out a long, tired sigh. "Do you think they'll believe us when we tell them?"

"They have to," Tom answered, "My dad saw the whole thing anyway. I guess they'll need our help if anything, to try to make sense of all this ..." He gestured to the ruined rubble of the Crematorium building.

Doc nodded and blew into his drink, watching the steam rise up in ghostly swirls. "Yeah. It's a lucky thing he came along when he did – with the fire engine. Saved our bacon that did."

"No luck involved, Doc," Tom disputed, remembering his burnt-out mobile phone... Tom had been puzzled at first when Dad had told him he'd received a text saying they were in danger, and to come straight to the Crem. He was even more taken aback when Dad had explained that the text had come from Tom's own mobile. Then Tom recalled the delay that Jazz had caused just on the edge of the grounds, before they had made their sprint across to the building earlier. He felt a bit guilty that he had suspected Jazz might be up to no good; he'd seen her messing with his phone. She had the presence of mind to contact Mr Allerton, knowing he was on duty.

Both boys peered out of the rear window as they heard the

churning-whirring sounds of helicopter blades. The chopper had landed just before the arrival of Doc's mum and dad. In fact, Mr Studd had spent a minute or two talking to one of the men who had disembarked from it, wearing a white protective suit and gloves, and a sort of surgical mask that covered the lower part of his face. Doc's dad told Mum to go and sit the boys in the car whilst he spoke to this man. Before Doc had been ushered away, he had glimpsed the white name tag of the man, which read: Professor Henry Creswell. Doc couldn't place it but he knew he'd heard the name before.

This same man had then busied himself surveying the scene and generally poking his nose into everything. He seemed to be in charge of a team of men and women who were examining the rubble and – particularly - the pile of old, charred bones. This group, who were all clad in the same clinical suits as Professor Creswell, had then carefully collected the bones and placed each into separate containers, marked: *Sterile. Keep at freezing point.* The strange little trinkets had also been gathered up and carefully boxed.

In addition, two huge crates with chains wrapped around them had been taken to the now derelict Crematorium building. The police officer who was guarding the ruins, looked at a sheet of paper that one of the men in white suits had given her, then nodded and stepped aside. From where they were sitting, Tom and Doc could just make out that the ghostly-looking people were dragging two huge objects – one into each crate, before lashing the heavy, shiny chains around the armoured boxes and snapping padlocks shut on them. As the things were heaved into the crates, the boys could just make out that they had several huge limbs, they were quite black, and their slick bodies reflected the flashing blue lights like weird mirrors. The huge helicopter had then flown off with the crates and the bones, like a grey, metallic bird of prey.

Neither boy spoke, not even to each other, about Jazz's unexplainable behaviour and her seeming control over the torrent of overhead water. They didn't know it, but shock was setting in, and the weariness they felt was not just down to lack of sleep.

The car door clicked open and a face loomed in, startling Tom and Doc so much that they nearly dropped their hot chocolate. The eyes were centred with pinpoints of red, caused by the glow of a police car's tail lights. "Hey … Steady on. I only came to check on you and see if you wanted any more hot drink." Doc's mum spoke reassuringly.

They both politely declined and Mrs Studd clicked the door closed again.

Doc's voice was shaky as he said, "You know, Tom, when I saw Mum's eyes just now, I thought -"

Tom interjected, "I know, mate – so did I. But it was just a reflection that's all."

Doc took off his glasses and rubbed his eyes, whispering: *"Those eyes … I don't think I'll ever forget those horrible eyes."*

Tom didn't know whether he meant Zeduza's – or Jazz's. Or both. Only Tom and Doc had seen that Jazz's eyes had transformed at that crucial, life-threatening moment. It wasn't anything that they could

183

make sense of right now, if ever.

But it did cross Doc's mind: *Back in the Crematorium, the fire-creature had taken Jazz over – possessed her. What if – just, what if – somehow, a part of Zeduza had remained with Jazz. Stained her D.N.A? Got into her blood?*

He had tried to shake the idea off as foolish, but it kept creeping into his brain, like a scorpion on the hunt.

Exhaustion finally enveloped the boys; they finished their drinks and closed their eyes. As they drifted off into a velvety sleep, the clouds parted briefly to reveal the full white moon. It looked down over all; a silent witness to a troubled night – then shrank back behind the scudding clouds, as if not wanting to see any more.

Epilogue

Charlotte has been told not to play near the old Crematorium. It isn't safe. A couple of months back there'd been all that trouble there, Mummy had told her. They still see lots of scientific-looking people visiting the place quite regularly.

Charlotte is a good girl and does what Mummy says. But today, Buster has slipped free of his leash, and he's run across the field behind their house. Charlotte loves this field; in the summer, it is always full of wild flowers of just about every colour you can imagine. On this dreary January day, it looks bare and windswept, but Charlotte knows the seeds will be waiting, all snuggled up in the ground, ready to stretch up and reach for the sun, come spring time.

"Bus – ter!" *Where is that naughty dog?* Charlotte giggles; Buster is always getting up to mischief.

Charlotte skips across the field as far as she dare, right to the edge, where the gap in the bushes leads to the grounds of the old Crematorium. Holding her breath, she peers through a gap in the foliage – a gap just the right size for a scruffy little black dog to sneak through.

"Buster?" She whispers now, as if frightened of waking the dead.

"Buster. Buster." And before she even knows it, she has popped through to the other side of the large, overgrown hedge.

185

"Buster, you silly boy. Come here!" she says sternly, although she is very pleased to see him, just a few metres along the bushes, sniffing in the hedge bottom. She is very glad he hasn't gone far into the grounds of the scary place; she doesn't like it here.

"Come here, Buster. We have to go back!" she half-whispers, half-shouts. Buster is fascinated by something that he has found in the grass and thistles that tangle in the lower branches of the bushes. Hesitantly, Charlotte walks over to the dog, looking all around her as she goes, just to make sure no ghosts get her. "What is it, Buster? What have you found?"

Buster stands with his tail sticking out horizontally at the back, and the fur on his back is sticking up in a straight line. His head is down and he stares intently at *something* in the hedgerow. As Charlotte draws nearer, she smells a horrid stink. "Buster! Are you sniffing at poo again?!" But then, although it does smell like poo, it is different too. It smells of rotten eggs and dead things.

Charlotte holds her nose and bends forward to see what Buster is so fascinated by. And her face beams with a smile of pleasure and surprise. There, in the hedge bottom, amongst all the dead twigs, lanky grass and nasty thistles of mid-winter, stands a beautiful flower. Its stem is half a metre high and the flower that blossoms on top is like nothing she has ever seen before. Multitudes of petals, of vibrant yellows, oranges and reds, project out like flames from a firework.

"Oh, Buster, you clever boy!" whoops Charlotte. "It's gorgeous. I must take it home to show Mummy!" She almost forgets about the bad

186

smell, as she reaches out her hand to stroke the pretty petals. As her fingertips touch the flower, Charlotte yelps in pain. She feels as if she has been burnt. When she looks at her fingers, she sees wicked red blisters.

Startled and hurt, she begins to sob loudly, and this makes Buster yap and yap in confusion. Charlotte turns and runs for the hole in the hedge, scrambling through and tearing her dress on a broken branch as she emerges on the other side. She runs and runs as fast as she can, and Buster scampers along behind her, with his tail between his legs.

From the place behind the hedge, where the flower is, Charlotte can hear a high-pitched screaming even worse than her own. But it is more of a screeching *howl* than a little-girl scream. And, to make matters worse, Charlotte thinks she can hear laughter mixed in with the terrible sound.

* * *

Midnight. A hedgerow on the outskirts of the ruined Crematorium. A hedgehog bustles and snuffles along. It sees a strange bloom swaying gently in the breeze. Instinctively, the little animal rolls into a ball, then scuttles off back the way it has come.

The strange flower nods in the wind, as if it knows its own power. And it is *aware* of others of its own kind. They have not yet broken through the earth; this flower is the first, but it will not be the last. Strange seeds wait patiently in the cradling soil for hundreds of metres around. Black, round seeds, that resemble miniature bullets.

Soon they, too, will emerge.

* * *

Charlotte peeps through the curtain from her bed. Her hand is still sore form the nasty flower earlier today. Mummy put antiseptic on her fingers and wrapped them in a nice soft bandage. She looks up at Mr Moon, high in his sky. She always says goodnight to Mr Moon, and he always smiles back at her. But tonight his face looks sad, and the rain running down the window makes him look like he's crying.

Charlotte closes her curtains quickly and dives under the duvet, where she wraps herself up tight, as snug as a seed in the ground.

In the far corner of Charlotte's room – in the shadows - stands a tall, muscular man, with cracked bronzed skin and a shaggy mane of hair. His wildly bearded old face contains two sharp, observant eyes.

He watches over the little one tonight.

THE END

Demons in the Dark
By John Clewarth

Sometimes, you wake up in the middle of the night, shaking with fear.

Those nightmares seem so *real,* don't they?

What exactly *is* it that casts that spooky shadow on your ceiling?

What *is* that sound coming from beneath your bed?

Dare you read *Demons in the Dark*?

Only the bravest in heart will turn the pages.

Believe me, there are things in this world that are best left unknown.

Unseen…

Released – June 2012 (Kindle e-book) and July 2012 (Paperback).

From Mauve Square Publishing.

Ninja Nan and the Trio of Trouble

By Annaliese Matheron

Ben, Kieran and the oldies are back for another adventure.
And this time their leaving Honeypot Grove and going on holiday.

The boys aren't alone.
Their little cousin, Sally, is coming along for the ride.

But even this can't dampen their spirits, not when Nan tells them that they are going on a two day Spy training course.

It's not long before Ben and Kieran are putting their newly acquired spy skills to the test as they find themselves in the middle of a mystery.

A mystery which surrounds Ben's evil nemesis, Mrs Gillespie.

When one old lady decides to do something nasty, it's up to Ben, Kieran and the group of geriatric spies, known as the NPS, to save the day.

Available Summer 2012

The Rainbow Animal

By Oliver Eade

Rachel hides her pet hamster, Waffles, in her dress pocket for his birthday present–a secret ride on a carousel animal at the local mall in Houston, Texas. Choosing the mysterious 'Rainbow Animal', she is transported to the strange world of Colorwallytown whose brightly-painted little inhabitants are about to go do battle with the black and white Dullabillies across the river…and all because of witches and fish!

Mistaken as the new Colorwally Military Advisor, the girl gets caught up in a paint war she cannot avoid. Worst of all, dreaded class nerd, Alec, whose parents are rumoured to be witches, appears to be on the opposing side until…

Available late spring 2012

Mauve
Square
Publishing

For information on these and other exciting
Mauve Square titles, visit our website:

www.mauvesquare.com